A QUICK S|

And Other *Popular* Out

Alternate Meanings of \

In Alphabetical and/or G\

Saucy Interpretations from A to Z
(and other suchlike blokey stuff)

"Pamela dear, are you holding something back from me?"

11958 TROW

by

MARK BARRY

TESTIMONIALS for the CLASSY LITERARY GENIUS CONTAINED WITHIN

"Mister Barry named a Salad after me last March, which is more than some backstabbers I could mention..."
JULIUS CAESAR

"I found his jokes on Emperor Penguins in bad taste..."
NAPOLEON BONAPARTE

"My son, *Little Hole in Rubber*, gave it to my sixth wife, *Pokes in Many Positions*, in our vacation tent, *I Heard It Through The Tepee Twine*..."
CHIEF SITTING BULL

"I have a copy in my pouch at boxing matches, always keeps the kids amused..."
SKIPPY THE BUSH KANGAROO

"As I was bathing in a Nottingham Forest river only yesterday, I'm quite sure that a copy of Mr. Barry's heartwarming book is what made Robin's tights all *a-quiver*..."
MAID MARION

"Samson uses them all the time to prop up pillars and hit hairdressers ...swears by them, actually..."
DELILAH

"I though his book so delightful, I contacted all 72 of the Virgins in the afterlife personally and each has valiantly agreed to service Mister Barry's infidel ass *before* they behead him (reasonable as always)..."
AYATOLLEH KHOMEINI

"I was disappointed to find no Sex with Nazis in it..."
COCO CHANEL

"I couldn't put it down. But then again, I can never put any real evil down..."
SATAN

First published in Great Britain in 11 January 2026

Copyright © Mark Gerard Barry 2026

The right of Mark Barry be identified as the Author of the Work
Has been asserted by him in accordance with the Copyright,
Designs and Patents Act 1988

CONTENTS

IT IS SO BRACING HERE AT CLIFTONVILLE.

Ace In The Hole

AARDVARK: A titmouse enforcer in the Norwegian underworld called *Vark*; nickname for Nick Park's yappy Cocker Spaniel in Aardman Animation studios: British Prog Rock band from 1970 on Deram Records who may have chosen their name because they'd always be first in music dictionaries even if they were last (or missing entirely) from your 1970 HMV shopping basket

AASVOGEL: Vogel The African Vulture worries that his posterior looks big in this

ABACUS: Agnetha, singer with the Swedish Pop Group ABBA, uses very strong language after not winning *Bellybutton of the Year* Award in 1974 whilst singing Waterloo in her cut-out Pink Heart Jumpsuit

ABBEY ROAD: four hung-over monks stagger across a Zebra crossing in St. John's Wood (one without shoes) singing about Toe Jam Football, Climbing in Through Bathroom Windows and Coming Together in an Octopus's Garden; unlikely NW8 name of a Beatles album from 1969

ABDICATOR: gym membership catering to He-Man Royals

ABDUCTEE: after a strenuous upper-body work-out at *Buff The Fluff* Muscle Emporium, Daffy Duck relaxes on the golf course

ABOVE AVERAGE: any LP placed on top of an Average White Band album

ABSENT MINDED: BBC shrinks open Keir Starmer's skull and make alarming discovery

ABSOLUTE CODSWALLOP: A North Sea Cod lands a Mohammed Ali type blow on the chip-shop owner trying to put him in a batter

ACE IN THE HOLE: whilst playing poker, gunslinger Billy The Kid looks up Sherriff Pat Garrett's posterior for a possible saviour card (preferably in Hearts) only to find Bob Dylan writing a song about knocking on a door in Heaven; World Poker Champion tells his wife he's about to come to bed

ACROSS THE UNIVERSE: after the success of their Netflix 4-Part Special, David and Victoria Beckham announce to the world that they're taking extreme measures to avoid press intrusion and are moving to a place where no paparazzi can ever reach them: Estate Agent in Margate offers first-time buyers apartments they can afford (sometime in the future, and perhaps a little off-grid)

ADVERSE WEATHER: advertisement telling poetry fans that a snowstorm has caused the cancellation of their rhyming evening

AEROSMITH: chocolate bar tries to hide its upper-crust origins by adopting a common surname; budget airline owned by Mrs. Smith of Tunbridge Wells

AESTHETICALLY PLEASING: a Stethoscope is pleased with her new look

AFFECT: Irish Judge curses in courtroom (uncharacteristically)

AFTER SHOCK: Californian woman who thought her husband had given her an orgasm the night before is disappointed to learn on the news the following morning that it was only an earthquake five miles away in a better neighbourhood: New York single lady is amazed when a male Manhattan one-night stand phones the next-day and even goes as far as remembering her name

AGONY AUNT: relative on your mother's side with bunions and/or haemorrhoids

AID and ABET: instead of food, clothing and essential supplies, a bungling United Nations committee sends humanitarian help to Africa in the form of one hundred self-assembly William Hill gambling shops

AIR TULIP: a fart in Amsterdam

ALI BABA: former American World Heavyweight Campion of the World Mohammed Ali accepts CIA assignment and goes undercover in Arabia to catch Forty Sheep Rustlers

ALIBI: former American World Heavyweight Campion of the World Mohammed Ali bids farewell to Forty Arabian Sheep Rustlers recently interred behind prison bars

ALIEN SEX FIEND: A disconsolate Buck Rogers sends a postcard home to his 21st Century family on Earth describing an alarming discovery he has made about his new wife on their Honeymoon night

ALL IS LOST: World's Most Intelligent Mensa Parents announce that their quirkily named love child (ALL) has gone missing in a Hounslow shopping mall

ALL RIGHT: command given by British National Front leader at their Christmas Party's game of Musical Chairs

THE ALLMAN BROTHERS BAND: hardcore Lesbian guitar group

ALMIGHTY DOLLAR: a Buck becomes a TV Evangelist

ALLOTA FAGINA: gynaecologist with a lisp explains to a female patient the sheer acreage of her nether regions

AMAZE BALLS: whilst rampaging across New York City with Fay Wray in his hand, King Kong catches a glimpse of his dangling undercarriage in the rear-view mirror of a 1933 Studebaker and is duly impressed; after a Saturday night on the tiles, French footballer Eric Cantona discovers a Manchester United tattoo in a place where he doesn't recall putting one

AMBULANCE CHASER: Thoroughbred Racehorse *Shergar* smokes a joint and sees a different winning post; Better Call Saul lawyer moves up in the legal world and starts to take cases that don't involve defending drug traffickers and rapists but instead people with suable injuries in A&E

AMMONIA: Kate Moss breaks a fingernail but downgrades her model rage into a single tantrum (a moan) before shouting out in agony the first and fifth letters of the alphabet (e and a)

AMULET: A Good Luck Token given by Estate Agents to renters seeking a reasonably priced flat in London

ANCILLARY: ants invade the set of Cilla Black's Blind Date

ANDROID: a female robot called Ann

ANGRY YOUNG MAN: every male University graduate everywhere at any time in history

ANKLE BRACELET: a Margate husband who chained his wife to the cooker for a year, claims to the police that new stainless-steel bonds were an Anniversary Gift, and you see this, because they were a generous three and half feet long

ANTIQUES ROAD SHOW: The Rolling Stones 2365 Final Tour (with Keith Richards as the only surviving original Rolling Stone)

ANTS IN HIS PANTS: Lord Of The Dance's Michael Flatley says his new musical extravaganza has been inspired by a recent location visit to the Amazon Rain Forest

APRIL SHOWERS – Post a three-way scene with Dr. Hardwick and Nurse DD of The Big O Research Facility on their latest film BANGERS And LASH - Porn Star April Whoppers is having a shower and can't get to the toilet fast enough so decides to use the facilities at hand

ARSE ABOUT FACE: The Editor of The Daily Mail discusses where he's putting what (and where) in his next surgical procedure

ARTIFACT: Jackson Pollock loved to drip dry; Pablo Picasso was a square; Salvador Dali's moustache was genuinely surreal

ARTY FARTY: Turner painting in Margate lets out a raspberry: Mona Lisa in Paris lets out a raspberry etc; British public gasps in wonder at a sensationally valid and artistically deep new exhibit in the London Turner Museum of Modern Art - Mark Barry's Margate flatulence captured live in a clear glass bottle and named "existential extension of succubus wombat third eye nebula" (or as is known locally - "Fart In A Bottle") [see also BOTTLED GAS]

ASCENDING THE RANKS: Manager is a cheese-making factory climbs up the corporate ladder by my lords it over

ASK MOTHER: red-headed father refers blond-haired son to his dark-haired wife re *origins of the species*

ASSUMPTION: claiming you know the size of a woman's derriere

ASTRONAUT: spaceman with a low IQ

ASTRONOMICAL EXPENSE: Russian Oligarch hosts his daughter's 18th birthday party on the Moon's Sea of Tranquility

ATONE FOR MY SINS: as a lover of music, I arrive in Purgatory for a multitude of transgressions (with the appropriate penance to be paid thereof as laid down by the Catholic Church) to find a set of headphones I must wear for 200 years with a single bum note playing through them

AU NATUREL: a cologne in a French Nudist Colony

AUCTIONEER: A Sotheby's Art Broker puts up a surprisingly affordable art-antiquity lot for sale (marked-down in price due to not being a complete pair) - a recently found *lug* belonging to Vincent Van Gogh

AUDITION ROLL CALL: an enterprising sandwich seller finds willing audience in Hollywood Casting Couch lounges

AUSPICE: a horse has a wee-wee

AUTHENTICATION NEEDED: Number 9 demands proof that Number 10 has a bigger schlong

AWARDS SHOW: Nurses in the USA stage a celebratory night out for staff of the Best Hospital ER Unit

AWESTRUCK: constantly amazed man gets another slap across the face

AWFULLY SORRY OLD BOY: an English Octogenarian son apologises to his uppercrust Centenarian father for past transgressions with the maid

AWKWARD AND SHY: Casanova gives his testicles nicknames

Bangers And Mash

BABOON: microphone used by Shaun The Sheep during interviews

BABY DRIVER: Highway Patrolman makes alarming discovery when he finds a 16-month-old infant is at the wheel of a Ferrari in Hollywood *researching a part*

BABYLON: name of Lon Chaney's first born

BABYPROOF: Alcohol rating for Gripe Water

BACHELORHOOD: a single Rapper joins the Harlem dating scene

BACKFLOW: a man with diahorrea points his Doctor to the problem

BACKLASH: S&M enthusiast affectionately names her fave whip

BACKLOG: A turd in reverse; a turd doing the Moon Walk

BAD BLOOD: Vlad The Impaler nursing a hangover; Dracula bites into the neck of Simon Cowell and immediately regrets the vintage

BAD TASTE: teeshirt on sale at a Hollies reunion concert that says "He Ain't Heavy, He's Anorexic

BAGGAGE RECLAIM: a Samsonite Briefcase sues Heathrow Airport for two decades of emotional trauma

BAGPUSS: Louis Vuitton's face on a Monday morning

BAGUETTE: long thin loaf of French bread seeks Camden Council funding for a sex change into a small leather bag

BAIKALITE: Delia Smith advises on the best way to baste a Solus Bulb

BAIL BOND: 007 sends an urgent e-mail to M from a Turkish Jail

BALDERDASH: British actor Patrick Stewart claims he can run after a ball faster than anyone else; Dwayne Johnson makes similar claim only 6000 miles away in America

BALLROOM BLITZ: How's-Your-Father Piccadilly Circus chorus dancers ignore sirens during World War II air raid and continue to give their male punters views of a more inspiring English Channel

BALLS TO THE WALL: Roger Waters of Pink Floyd, takes his 1979 double-album magnum opus a little too far one night during a live performance by committing to nail his testicles to the stage show

BANANA SPLITS: a tearful and emotionally bruised Banana divorces her once Peach of a husband citing his womanising ways with that slut of a Kumquat in a nearby Fruit Bowl (Hannah Banana is also suing for custody of their two Californian Raisin children)

BANGERS AND MASH: staff conduct an orgy at a Maris Pipers potato depot

BARBECUE BEEF: Purchase line outside a Californian Patel Store as the company puts on sale the first *Barbie Doll* with a lifelike penis beneath its pink jacket and skirt

A BARREL OF LAUGHS: A vat of Guinness has a fit of the giggles

BATMAN: David Attenborough smiles gamely as he toboggans down a mountain of excrement in a Malaysian cave whilst holding his nose with one hand and an ammonia-proof microphone in the other (see also ROBIN)

BEACHHEAD: Baywatch Lifeguard administers an emergency procedure

BEAVERPELT: Topless Model throws her recent gathered-up Brazilian at her cheating boyfriend

BEDROCK: Dwayne Johnson wakes up with an erection

BEE'S KNEES: honey-making insect sings his own praises (see also CAT'S PAJAMAS)

BEEFCAKE: M&S Confectionist finds a Creamy Phallus in her Black Forest Gateau

BEEFEATERS: Vegetarian protest group chained to a McDonald's Kiosk; a group of holidaying ladies board a Chippendales Tour Bus in Las Vegas

BEGETTING: Bumble Bee on his honeymoon finds his wife is a goer

BELOW DECKS: Dexter the Serial Killer looks down at his sawed-off junk and rather wishes he hadn't so pissed the night before

BEND THE KNEE: one of five initiation rituals performed when joining the Margate Senior Citizens Bowling Club (the Chairman can't remember the other four); Sky TV program's popular catch phrase; arthritic pensioner offers up her excuse for not being able to play basketball with street kids

BETAMAX: Happy Hour at Madame Maximum's Dominatrix S&M Parlour

BI-FOCALS: A pair of Ray Bans that swings both ways

BIG BEN: Mrs. Hur's standard response when asked how potent her husband's biblical staff is

BIG GIRL'S BLOUSE: a weedy young man – or a young man made weak at the knees by the excitement of the filled-up blouse

BIG JUGS: dual entries in an *Oversized Pottery* competition

BIJOU: see (LONDON) CAVE DWELLERS

BIMONTHLY: Labour Party Activist describes how many partners he/she sleeps with every two weeks (a cut back since the every-two-days scandal of February 2025)

BISEXUAL: a Binary Coder at Apple discovers lovemaking; pensioners wave goodbye to more than their freedom when entering a retirement home: Max Bygraves explains to his wife his need for two-way sex of a different kind

BLACK and WHITE (see also BREAKING BAD): Pop Singer Michael Jackson declares that he likes children no matter what the colour

BLATANT LIE: every time Kamala Harris deigned to open her mouth in the Presidential Race of November 2024

BLUETOOTH: a sex-mad Molar

BOBBY DAZZLER: Actor Robert Pattinson driving in Los Angeles at night with his full beams on

BOBCAT: William Shakespeare, Bob Dylan's precocious Siamese cat, refuses to acknowledge that it once wee-wee'd on its owners 1966 Leopard-Skin Pillbox Hat in a literal hissy fit about a complete lack of chewy treats in her window bowl while her moody keeper was away writing overly-long and impenetrable lyrics to songs about dodgy rainy-day women and hipsters with tambourines

BODY BLOW: Not understanding why's he's there, Former President Donald Trump publicly snorts cocaine off his wife's bare chest live on TV during Impeachment and Tax Evasion Hearings

BODY SHOP: Governor Arnold Schwarzenegger offers to have on-camera mano-a-mano sex with his personal trainer as a first prize in a new bid to bring more tourists into California: London boutique that sells high-quality cadavers (none of your foreign muck)

BODY WASH: written in large block capitols, wife leaves a subtle hint on a Post-It note stuck to the kitchen fridge-door to her obsessed Squash-Playing husband

BOLLOCKS: Official title for British Testicles after October 1977

BONAPARTE: Napoleon's nickname for his Poteau of Love when away from Joséphine

BOOTY CALL: an iPhone rings in the trunk of a Maserati

BOTTOM LINE: street-artist Banksy paints a line of unemployed immigrants across the arse of a sleeping King Charles in Highgrove in non-washable ink and then posts the location of his newest creation for art hunters looking to make a few bob on eBay (courtesy of Royal benevolence)

BREAKING BAD: Sony/Epic Records Music Executive uses lump mallet on a Michael Jackson CD when he finds out that the singer *really* likes children of all colours

BREXIT: a this-way-out sign on a toilet door in Antarctica (Brrr)

BRICK LANE: Superman (aka Clark Kent) describes the first time he was sexually aroused by Lois at the Daily Planet's wet teeshirt weekend

BRING AND BUY SALE: Cockimus's table at the Colosseum Bizarre selling used but well maintained Dildos for Roman Gladiators

BRISTOL CHANNEL: Page 3 Model loses an implant on her daily swim

BROTHERS GRIMM: Mark Darcy and his brother Tom are forced to wear hideous reindeer jumpers at a family Christmas party (though visiting TV type Bridget Jones thinks they're cute)

BROTHERS AND SISTERS GRIMM: Boris and Rachel Johnson contemplate Brexit

BUBBLEGUM: scientists put a set of dentures in a vacuum

BUCCANEAR: a Novel and an Earlobe have an affair

BUCK'S FIZZ: Captain Rogers of the 25th Century describes the first time he came on an alien

BUCKING THE TREND: a cheap pulp-fiction paperback demands a dustjacket

BUCKET SHOP: a lovestruck Spade hangs out all summer long by a tourist shop to get a glimpse of his big-handled sweetheart

BUDDHIST RETREAT: a monk notices his hairline is going back while his belly goes in the opposite direction

BUFFALO BILL: Monica Lewinsky describes to a grand jury the marauding nature of President Clinton's campaign contributions

BUDGIE SMUGGLERS: a huge pair of testicles writes to the Home Office about being hidden away and the cramped overhung conditions he must work with

BUGBEAR: a caterpillar complains to Mowgli that Baloo of *The Jungle Book* doesn't appreciate his efforts at satisfying coitus

BUM DEAL: Andrew Mountbatten is advised by Ghislaine Maxwell on prison etiquette

BUM NOTE: Octave suffering from persistent flatulence; a lone piano ping sails out of Beethoven's arse during another one of his rants about hearing aids

BUNNY BOILER: Bugs Bunny's plumbing business; enterprising new gas-boiler company targets the lady of the house by naming their latest appliance after a scene in the famous movie and painting Glenn Close on the side cowling behind a shower-curtain with a knife

BUOYED UP: Jimmy Savile OBE gets excited as he bounces an 8-year-old "Jim'll Fix It" contestant on his knee with the lad's parents watching in the crowd: BBC Top of the Pops presenter lives up to the word *vile* in his surname

BUSH TUCKER TRIAL: an Australian woman with an unusually hairy minge tries out a new pantyhose that discreetly hides excess protrusion

GEORGE BUSH: American President who refused a Brazilian at Vidal Sassoon's 'Shave One Poonanny and Get The Other One Free' Spa Day; hedge in George Michael's front garden: Susan George's pubic region

BUZZWORD: A Bumble Bee writes his Autobiography

Constructive Feedback

CAESAR SALAD: Roman Dictator watches his weight after being too slow to notice recent stabbing in the back

CALLOUS BEHAVIOUR: Former British Prime Minister Theresa May so upset by Conservative Party skulduggery that she vows to work as a street labourer until her hands are raw and bloodied like her colleagues hearts

CANARY ISLANDS: popular holiday destination to pick up *fit birds* that aren't necessarily from the Finch Family

CAN'T BUY A THRILL: a Budgie bemoans his seedless love life

CARAVAN: Van Morrison covers himself in Caramel

CARPET MUNCHERS: ladies who prefer a good Axminister rug to beef chow mien

CAT'S PAJAMAS: best long johns ever owned by Catherine The Great

CAVE DWELLERS: London housing market upgrade; and/or *bijou accommodation* in a cliff location near Dover

CEILING STARS: Name of the Canteen at Paranal Observatory in the Atacama Desert in Northern Chile

CHAIN STORES: Bicycle shops that only sell one product

CHASTE WOMEN: Casanova describes the activities of his average Saturday Night

CHEAP AS CHIPS: an increasingly irrelevant phrase

DICK CHENEY: former US Vice President regrets getting 13th Century Chainmail surgically attached to his penis

CHEWY BAR: between-takes snack for a Stars War character

CHIEF WHIP: Sitting Bull's nickname for his todger

CHIP BUTTY: Boris Johnson is alarmed to find an old sandwich from 2015 stuck up his arse

CHOMPING AT THE BIT: Mark Zuckerberg eats his own computer for dinner

CIVIL WAR: American and Russian armies play chess on a submarine between Nuclear exchanges

CLEANING CADDIES: Rory McIlroy turns a Hosepipe on rival Golf Carts

CLIMB DOWN: having reached the summit, Edmund Hillary explains to Tenzing Norgay how to get off Mount Everest

CLOUD NINE: an After Eight Mint describes exceptional sex with a Turkish Delight; latest addition to the Cloud family

COCK 'O THE HOOP: flea in miniature circus jumps over his own penis

COCKLES AND MUSCLES ALIVE ALIVE-O: Bodybuilders in Mr. Universe competition compare Dick functionality vs. Ab size

COCKTAIL HOUR: Working Penises take a break in The Beaver Bordello

CODPIECE: seafood flashes his cock to a mortified mollusc; fish sees too many John Wayne movies and begins to wear a holster

COLD COMFORT: an armchair beside a fridge full of Cornetto's in Iceland

COME AGAIN: the Virgin Mary queries the Three Wise Men on their prognosis; title of the exciting sequel to the New York Times bestseller "Climax: An Orgasm's Memoirs"

COMING SOON: film trailer for "Debbie Does Dallas 6"; seventy-three-year-old man makes big promises in bed to a 23-year-old glamour model

COMPLETE BLANK: standard response from Republican politicians when asked if they know anyone whose poor; standard response from Republican politicians when asked if they know what's inside Donald Trump's manbag

(A) COMPLETE WANKER: Middle Eastern masturbator keeps to his promise and instead of just one girl, shoots his load all over the Sheik's entire Harem; all-party negotiator for Brexit; Tom Cruise espouses the wonders of Scientology – a cult religion made up by a Science Fiction writer to screw money out of gullible young people

COMPOUND INTEREST: on compassionate shore leave after nine months in a nuclear submarine, US sailor Private John 'Com' Companelli tells a Moulin Rouge pole dancer in Paris of his urgent desire to engage in American/French relations in one of the nightclub's backstage VIP suites

COMPUTER: a timesaving device primarily used for time-wasting activities (written by someone else)

COMMON LAW LOVE: A Californian lawyer is struck by lightning on his way to Big Yun's Sushi Bar and thereafter swears to defend the poor and not Kim Kardashian's emotionally traumatized iPhone that fell on the pavement for four seconds during an exclusive Vogue photo shoot of her bottom

CONCRETE EVIDENCE: Don Corleone's lawyer finally produces missing witness in high profile Mafia trial (a bit worse for wear)

CONCURRENT CIRCLES: today, two pickpockets on a tandem bicycle navigating a roundabout

CONSISTENT PORTIONS: wives of Wets End chefs confirm that their husbands regularly delivery in the bedroom

CONSTRUCTIVE FEEDBACK: Bricklayer describes sex with a Fender Telecaster that had electrical issues

CONTENTS: Pale Faces erect false Tepees

CONUNDRUM: Irish thief *Connor Underwood* steals part of U2's rhythm section

COOKIE CUTTERS: McVitie's Digestive Biscuit buys a lawnmower

COOLING RACKS: contestants at the World Biggest Breasts Convention enjoy a swim in a nearby plunge pool

COURT JESTER: Lawyer representing Harvey Weinstein; Lawyer representing Sean P Diddy Combs

CRAB STARTERS: after a visit to a Bombay massage parlour, a tourist finds that something other than Masala was on the menu

CREAM PUFFS: Two members of Eric Clapton's 60ts supergroup finally admit that blizzards of drugs made them gay (no names please)

CREAMY COLESLAW: an unhinged Cabbage masturbates on a Side Salad

CRIMINAL PARTS: Dr. Frankensteins Creature discovers from his maker why he keeps thinking of pickpockets and thievery as he leaves the lab

CROWN JEWELS: unimportant pieces of carbonised glass of no monetary value whatsoever; Englishman's body parts of the utmost importance and value (also applies to men of many other nationalities and religions); Prince Andrew alerts British hospital staff on a no-go area during routine physical check-up; see also FUZZY WUZZY

CRUDE OIL: a tin of Castrol GTX is shockingly rude to an OPEC conference delegate

CUBBYHOLE: Boy scout's makeshift outdoor loo

CUNNILINGUS: the National airline carrier for Ireland, Aer Lingus, announces a new airline tailoring to the needs of Irish Women

CURIOSITY KILLED THE CAT: weary of cartoon character Tom (the cat) leering into his skirting board hole for a chance to clobber him, Jerry (the mouse) finally loses it and puts a bullet in the moggy's head

Don't Walk On The Grass

DAILY MIRROR: Tuesday takes a long hard look at its midweek status

DAIRY BREEDS: sexually voracious bar of Cadbury's chocolate

DAKOTA FANNING: after an extreme heatwave, an entire Minnesota City turns on the AC

DAMAGE APPRAISAL: Pompeii Estate Agent 'Lava, Lava and More Lava' give gloomy property–prices forecast after Mount Vesuvius has a 'slight' eruption in 79AD

DAMN THE TORPEDOES: Mother of 14 Catholic Children, Mrs. Brenda Legalot lets her husband Shafting Seamus know of her feelings as he lets another one fly

DAMNED ATTRACTIVE: Lucifer admires his new fiery red suit in the mirror

DAMPENER ON IT: an entire beach of Italian Men pour packets of Salt Peter into their swimming trunks as Sophia Loren exits the Sea

DAMSEL IN DISTRESS: Rapunzel frets over hair extension bought on eBay; Rapunzel kills a split-end in a temper-tantrum when she finds out her knight is late because he's still shining his armour so he can see his face and teeth in it; Lady Guinevere pines for Lancelot's swordplay

DANCES WITH CHICKENS: rejected name for a Kevin Kostner movie

DEAD AHEAD: a British road sign advises that graveyard is nearby

DEALERSHIP: a cruise for gamblers banned from Las Vegas

DEATH AND TAXES: Autobiography of Ghengis Khan's accountant

DEEP SLEEP: Bunk Bed found sitting on the silt of the Mariana Trench seven miles below the sea's surface

DEF CON ONE: trick played on a hard-of-hearing nuclear-weapon

DEMEANOR BY DA MINOR: Midget New York Rapper expresses his anger

DENIES ALL KNOWLEDGE: Former American President Joe Biden's standard response to any questions on money or any other subject for that matter (see also WORDS FAIL ME)

DICK WAD: Harvey Weinstein's penis reports theft of its strap-on wallet; Willy proudly displays other attribute worth standing up for

DIDDLY SQUAT: legendary Chess Vocalist and Guitarist Bo Diddley demonstrates his favourite daily exercise position; farm owned by Jeremy Clarkson

THE DIDDLY SQUATI: Poorer relatives of The Dothraki in Game Of Thrones

DILLY DALLIES: 75-year *Dowager Dilly Dunblowing* rides her husband a little longer in the hope of an orgasm

DIME STORE COWBOY: John Wayne Western made for 10 Cents

DIPLOMATIC IMMUNITY: During a rare TV interview and having previously pleaded lack of knowledge when asked about the irreparable harm done to children abducted by Cartel Gangs who crossed into Texas when she was the appointed Border Tsar for 4 years, former White House Democrat and Vice President Kamala Harris suddenly remembers a handy law when asked again about it during a Joe Rogan podcast

DINGBAT – *Maniacal laughter ring-tone* on Robin's mobile phone (with added echoes from the Bat Cave for more effect)

DIRE STRAITS: convention celebrating curvy women mistakenly invites tall women to speak to delegates; choppy part of the Mediterranean Sea; British Rock Band who turn out to be not so bad after all and aren't broke either

DISADVANTAGED YOUTH: Rock Band at Harvard University

DISC JOCKEY: British DJ Tony Blackburn holding Led Zeppelin's "Houses Of The Holy" LP are both Cellotaped to Red Rum's saddle in the 1973 Grand National

DIZZY HEIGHTS: 22 fashion models on the viewing deck at the top of the Empire State Building [see also LEG ROOM]

DR. HARDWICK: Lead character in the famous porn sequel "Debbie Comes Again In Dallas" where Dr. Hardwick of the Big O Research Clinic helps Nurse Double-D overcome her fear of pleasure

DON'T WALK ON THE GRASS: customised doormat outside Bob Marley's house

DOUGHNUT: a sliced-pan of bread and a macadamia exchange monosyllabic nicknames as they pass on the street

DOWN TO THE WIRE: Queen of England stoops for the first time in her life, only it's to pick up the BLU RAY edition of her favourite American Cop Show

DOW-JONES AVERAGE: During their highly acrimonious alimony trial, the plaintive Miss Margarita Consuela Jones of Columbia, describes the bedroom acumen of the accused, Lord Reginald Bosenquet Dow of Lowbrow Manor, in unfavourable market terminology

DUBIOUS CHOICES: Dubliner Mark Barry asks a Dark Horse to dance at a Local Hop

DUBSTEP: form of Reggae that originated in Ireland's Capitol City

DUGOUT: Douglas Farter is ordered to exit his Trench due to rear-end issues

DULY NOTED: Julie Andrew's Diary

DUMP RUN: Usain Bolt in need of an outside lavvy

Egg And Chips

EAGLES: American Country Rock Band trapped in IKEA Thurrock where they find out the hard way that you check out any time you like, but you can never leave

EASTERN PROMISE: Belly Dancer Mimi Le Sizzle claims she can fry an egg on her abs during her dance of passion but draws the line at beans and mushrooms

EFFETE: Irishman curses his huge clodhoppers as he puts his foot in it once again

EGG and CHIPS: nickname for a Free-Range Chicken and Home-Grown Potato Celebrity Couple

ELMER THE ELEPHANT: Loony Tunes character *Elmer Fudd* has an identity crisis and craving for peanuts

EMERGENCY ROOM: tasting department in Dublin's Guinness Brewery

END RESULT: horse in the Grand National with a flabby bottom secures a surprise win

ENVIRONMENTALLY FRIENDLY: a Gastro Pub Owner's excuse to the Police for his sozzled customers pissing on nearby trees

EPSOM SALTS: A packet of SAXA goes to the racetrack

EQUAL RIGHTS FOR WOMEN: something a woman wants - as long as she's getting her own way

EXISTENTIAL THREATH TO ALL LIFE ON EARTH: an Irishman discovers there's only one bag left in his tea caddy

EYE CANDY: Scarlett Johansson tours Cadburys in an Avengers catsuit; A Rowntree's Fruit Pastille with exceptional cleavage

EYE FOR AN EYE: a not-very-smart one-eyed Cyclops offers a mirror a gift

Fruity Pots

FACIAL RECOGNITION SOFTWARE: cheating-on-your-wife alerting-app ruled out by all-male US Congress (later ruled in by the wives of the same all-male Congress)

FAMILIARITY BREEDS CONTEMPT: a close-knit patch of Cabbages decide to grow a Carrot, but he turns out to be a little cunt

FANNY MAGNET: Mary Berry, Britain's favourite lady chef, announces a new line for Christmas gifts, magnetized clitorises for your fridge

FATHER OF PSYCHOANALYSIS: Sigmund Freud phones his Dad

FATTENING FOR FROGS: an *all-you-can-eat* McDonalds on the Champ Elysees

FAUX PAS: French Dad derided as a poorly outfitted lingerie model

FATWA: Wa, the Muslim Gym Instruction, starts up a Weight-Watchers class for Islamic terrorists in Watford

FEATHERBRAIN: Daffy Duck ponders the meaning of life

FED-EX: FBI agent's estranged wife

FELINE GRACE: Grace Kelly's cat on To Catch A Thief

FELLATIO: receptionist's name at a Roman Centurian Baths; nickname for a Centurian's pipe-cleaner

FERRARI: an aerodynamic but garishly dressed phallus on the M25

FIRE SALE: Lucifer organises a Bring and Buy table in Hades

FISH PEOPLE: congregation at the marriage of a Salmon and a Haddock; Kate Bush's record label

FIVE BUCKS: A British Rock Band rename their group DOWN TIME after meeting five cheerleaders in an American Bar

FLASH IN THE PAN: TV Celebrity Chef shocks audience when he shoots his ejaculating penis into a bowl of caramelized Crème Brûlée in protest at its lack of custard filling

FLAT PACK: something you bought to save money, but to save your sanity, you pay someone else to assemble it for more than it cost you to buy in the first place

FLAYGRANT VIOLATION: a Human Resources tribunal at a whip factory

FLIPPING BURGERS: CIA agent takes a course in *turning* Quarter Pounders away from Communism

A FOOL AND HIS MONEY: a banker on a slot machine in Las Vegas

FOREWORD: emotional outburst by Tiger Woods on the 17th Hole as he sees his wife's divorce lawyer throw something at him

FOUR WEDDINGS AND A FUNERAL: Hugh Hefner receives an alarming tarot card reading on his physical future at Playboy Mansion

FOX AND HOUND: James Bond and Miss Moneypenny on their first date

FRAGRANT ROSE: Petunia regrets a back-garden date with a farting suitor

FRANCHISE: St. Francis of Assisi goes rogue and reads a 'How To' manual on brand recognition

FREEBIES: a hive offers up its produce for naught

FREEDOM OF INFORMATION: bugger the truth, here's what we want you to know: knowledge that doesn't cost you anything

(GIVING A) FRENCH: game lady who engages in mouth-to-mouth with something thick, arrogant and vaguely smelling of cheese

FRENCH FRIES: A bag of chips enrols in a Parisienne course on erotic kissing

FRETBOARD: a Bulletin area in a moaner's convention

FRIDGE MAGNET: sexually vivacious lamb chop tries to seduce an underage Cornetto in M&S Food Hall back to his 'cool pad'

FRIENDS WITH BENEFITS: all your pals are on the dole

FRIENDSHIP: Jennifer Aniston and David Schwimer meet unexpectedly on a cruise

FRILLY KNICKERS: Annual Board Meeting for M&S underwear thieves

FRINGE ELEMENT: a Magnesium particle (from the Period Table) gets his 12th haircut

FRONTIER: a woman with unfeasibly large breasts rest her assets on a balcony in the upper part of a cinema

FRUIT BASKET: a bowl of Cherries in an Insane Asylum

FRUITY POTS: Kylie Mare Rouge (aka Fruity Pots), sexy sister of Cambodian leader Pol Pot; infamous lip-synching dancing troupe in Pol Pot's Kampuchean nightclub "Sucky-Sucky Five Bucks"

FULL METAL JACKET: lady worries about her first night with a Vietnam drill sergeant when he turns up on their first date with an unusual blazer

FULLY LOADED: Michael Parkinson tries to interview celebrity chef Keith Floyd and notorious actor Oliver Reed but finds they've been to the bar beforehand

FUNNY FARM: a Dairy where all the cows are stand-up comedians

FUZZY WUZZY: a Jewish wife of 45-years states that while she can remember where every shoe-shop in London, New York and Paris is, her mind regularly goes blank when asked to locate her husband's pubic region (see also CROWN JEWELS)

Good Vibrations

G-SPOT: profoundly mythical place most men haven't found in thousands of years (never thought to ask either)

GAINED WEIGHT: 200-year-old skeleton pleased with reading on a museum weighing scales

GALWAY BAY OYSTERS: Celtic aphrodisiacs that raise libido and provide a great view during out-door sex at one and the same time (see also A QUICK SHUFTY)

GANGRENE: an Irish Drug Cartel; Eton school dinner made with week-old cabbage

GASLIGHT: Thomas Edison admits that a severe case of flatulence gave him the inspiration for the electric bulb

GENDERFLUID: Hotel Cleaners describe deposits left by the toilet seats of their single male guests

GENERAL KNOWLEDGE: soldier who can name every 5-star commander whose ever lived

GENIUS: Arabian conjuror agrees to leave his lamp and grant three wishes to absolutely everyone

GEORGE BUSH: American President who refused a Brazilian at Vidal Sassoon's 'Shave One Poonanny and Get The Other One Free' Spa Day; hedge in George Michael's front garden: Susan George's pubic region

GET UP AND GO: Casanova's post-coital Mantra

GLADIATOR: Roman Centurion *Hung Wellicus* describes how pleased he was at his first orgy in the Colosseum and how he also enjoyed going down on Queen Cleopatra's Egyptian Garden

GLUTTEN FREE: complimentary biscuit at Wheat Farmers Annual Hoedown

GOALPOST: a mailman watches the World Cup

(THE) GOAT: lone farmyard animal claims to have the best sheep-shagging seduction techniques

GOBBLEDYGOOK: a Turkey who becomes a spy

GODFATHER: Universe controller tweaks his latest dubious invention – the Mafia Boss – to be imbibed with fine Italian clothes and cuisine

GODMOTHER: the woman the Creator of all things is more scared of

GODSON: an offspring who keeps out of the way of both parents

GOGGLEBOX: a coffin for a Plasma TV

GOLDILOCKS: a set of keyholes covered in wee wee

GOLFING BAG: 92-year-old lady goer has a swing at a 93-year-old business tycoon in a Florida Clubhouse

GOLFING TEE: a nice cuppa for both nonagenarians after their exertions

GOOD TO GO: a phrase uttered by the Archbishop of Canterbury after 96 days of constipation

GOOD VIBRATIONS: a 6.5 Earthquake in San Francisco is heard to be destroying buildings to the dulcet tones of a Beach Boys song; A wife hears her next-door neighbour enjoying herself on the washing machine

GOUT: Australian phrase that describes going out for a Fosters

GOYA: plural of non-Jewish Goyish men

GRABHOOKS: Captain Hook's long-suffering wife

GRACELESS: Grace Kelly minus a bra

GRAMATICALLY INCORRECT: a noun makes a lurid pass at an adverb

GRANDAD: an old man who will only express own views on the world in his back garden Man Cave with the door locked; in awe of Grandma; worries about the viability of Greyhound Racing come the Apocalypse in 2058

GRANDMA: an old woman who smells of Pot Pourri, Kindness and Home

GRANDMA and GRANDAD: people who've raised children of their own and therefore at the end of the day have the good sense to hand grandchildren back; old people who claim to know better than you, but don't (but you suspect they do, and they can't ever, ever, ever know that)

GRANNY TAKES A TRIP: One of the investigative gang in The Thursday Murder Club discovers LSD as an advanced method of sleuthing

GRANOLA: your Grandad and Gran's jukebox

GREAT BALLS OF FIRE: nickname Jerry Lee Lewis gave his gonads after a weekend at his cousins

GREAT EXPECTATIONS: a Barmaid is led to believe by a regular that his perpendicular feelings for her will remain pointed come closing time

GREATEST LOVE OF ALL: Casanova looks in a mirror

GREY AREA: female senior citizen (Rosie) doubts that her 75-year-old Internet date (Rick) is being truthful about his hair colour

GRIZZLY APPEARANCE: after escaping London Zoo, an American Bear then waits patiently outside Hampstead's Bannatyne Health Club and Spa for an appointment with their top manicurist; Baloo The Bear worried about his image in The Jungle Book

GROUNDBREAKING: Elephant in a Tutu rehearsing Swan Lake

Hard Rock Café

HAGRID: Harry Potter character; old woman whose just removed 35 years of facial stubble with a used wire brush

HAM AND EGGS: a bad actor plays six free-range eggs

HAN SOLO: a space mercenary has a hand shandy in a galaxy far, far away

HAND-RAIL: British Rail introduces cheaper but more physically challenging mode of train transport for cash-strapped commuters

HAND SHANDY: Coca-Cola invents a new fizzy drink that has a disastrous launch due to bottle contents

HANNAH BANANA: see BANANA SPLITS

HAPPY FAMILIES: a myth made up by American card companies the same day they invented Christmas

HAPPY HOUR: *Three O'Clock* wins 1-million on the Lotto

HARD-HITTING FEMINIST: Germaine Greer repeatedly smacks the erect phallus of a Sun journalist with her school ruler

HARD ON THE FEET: as she's dragged across her partner's extended nether regions on stage during Swan Lake, a ballerina wonders is that crotch padding she's feeling on her plimsolls or his excitement at the part

HARD ROCK CAFÉ: where black male porn stars go for a relaxing latte after a long and hard day on set (see also ROCK ARCHIVES)

HEART RATE: unscrupulous surgeon sells a patient's major body part for a dirt-cheap price on eBay (includes VAT)

HEART TO HEART: Online WhatsApp call between two Aortas

HEN NIGHT: chickens enjoy a stripper dressed as a Rooster

HERD IMMUNITY: a Buffalo sues the State of Wyoming for lack of privacy in a recent cattle drive

HERETIC: women who say Star Wars is unimportant and men should get over it (see also HERESY)

HERESY: see HERETIC (as a matter of urgency)

HETRO: reclaimed manliness; a reclaimed and upcycled decorator from the 70ts rebranded and given a new lick of environmentally friendly distressed look chalk paint

HIGH AND MIGHTY: a lone rose blooms on the summit of Everest

HIGH END: giraffe's posterior; the place where Kim Kardashian's bottom meets her G-string

HIGH END FURNITURE: Freddie Mercury's double bed on the summit of Kilimanjaro

HIGH FIDELITY: Edmund Hilary conquers Mount Everest only to find a 1953 Stereogram already set up on its peak

HOCKEY STICKS: irate ice-rink enthusiasts find their favourite game equipment has been glazed with honey overnight by beekeepers

HOCUS POCUS: a coven of witches have a shagging competition to see which one can penetrate the deepest

HOGGING THE ROAD: Macy the Aberdeenshire Sow behind the wheel of a Range Rover post discovery of her husband Angus's farmyard infidelities

HONEYMOON PERIOD: the first two weeks of marriage, thereafter it's pistols/daggers at dawn (see QUICK SHUFTY)

HONOURABLE DISCHARGE: Chief Justice does a wee wee under his desk whilst banging his gavel

(IT'S ALL GONE) HORRIBLY WRONG: having just chin-wagged with God, Moses comes down from the top of Mount Sinai and hands his people ten instructions on how to avoid this scenario and go in the opposite direction; Director of "Caligula" gives the press a review of his own film

HORSE WHISPERER: attending a *Stud Sensitivity Seminar* after complaints of largesse in the stable-boudoir, Red Rum tries a new approach with this week's 128th mare

HOT FLAMING DESIRE: a Barbeque Steak admires itself in a pocket mirror

HOTTER THAN JULY: stripper called August who raises concerns about a fellow pole dancer to her immediate left whose libidinous routines with ice-lollies in Big Jock's All Seasons Tits 'n' Ass Bar in Kansas may be making punter's bra dollars soggy and unusable; stripper called August tries to outdo her pal to the immediate left

HOUSE MINORITY WHIP: privileged politician with a truly tiny schlong

HOUSE OF COMMONS: working-class family squats in a semi-detached home in Camden after eviction by a Westminster slum landlord

HUBCAP: Stetson Hat for a White Wall Tyre

HULA HOOPS: KP Snacks enters the lucrative Hawaiian sex-toys marketplace by creating the world's first edible penis rings

HUMM-V: after sleeping with an entire SEAL team in the Barracks shower area, actress and part-time belly dancer Va-Va-Voom Lust Bucket's contentment can be heard for miles

HUNG OVER: to the amazement of visitors, a bored African Elephant dangles his penis over a Safari truck at one of the ladies within

HUSBAND: the Hus Family Folk Quintet; a man who clears all opinions through his wife; Majorie Hus, dutiful spouse of Major Thumper Hus, declares his big band drum is off-limits after her eighth pregnancy

It's Not Unusual

I LEFT MY HEART IN SAN FRANCISCO: Tony Bennett realises at SFO check-in that he's left more than his wallet in the California airport; checking up his sleeve, a card cheat realises he left behind a crucial suit card on his annual vacation to a Vegas Poker Tournament

I SAW THE LIGHT: Todd Rundgren wonders at the marvels of a 40-watt bulb

ICE SHAVER: name of a barbers in Alaska

IDIOT SAVANT: Sav the Ant complains incessantly about his derogatory Christian Name

IKEA: a hugely efficient flat-pack Swedish hotel and/or prison building where you check in, but you can never leave; where Laura Ashley is doing hard time for crimes against curtains

ILL WILL: recently disclosed title of Jill Biden's Pre-Nup (wife of former incapacitated President Joe Biden); excuse given by Will Smith's agent when asked if the slap-happy actor will host the next Oscars

I'M ON THE OUTSIDE LOOKING IN: a victim of Harvey Weinstein's sexual assaults in hotel bathrooms stands outside his prison cell, smiling; British Politician David Cameron describes Brexit and most Prime Minister weekdays

IMPORTANT MAN: Victoria Secret Male Model with a speech impediment is found to have a low sperm count

IN CAHOOTS: Happiest town in Canada

THE 'IN' CROWD: Christmas Party for Holiday Inn staff

INFINITY POOL: discovering that steel chains have been put around both of his ankles by an overzealous trainer, British Olympian diver Tom Daley fears that he'll never escape the 10-metre platform now (even on Sundays)

IN THE MOOD: Glenn Miller's wife texts her husband that she's open for business

INADMISSABLE EVIDENCE: in a highly sensitive court case, a vagina accuses a penis of broken penetration-promises made prior to disastrous first-date intercourse

INALIENABLE RIGHTS: A left-turn sign accuses a right-turn sign of hogging road directions

INBREEDING: Parents come home from the opera to find their male babysitter and teenage daughter engaging in some bountiful European liaisons of their own

INCESSANT INTERRUPTIONS: a Durex complains to its willy owner about too-many incoming calls

INCIDENTAL CHARGES: a Telegraph Pole enjoys an occasional orgasm

INCITING A RIOT : actress and babe Sidney Sheridan enters a Town Hall protest about inappropriate office attire wearing only a bikini

INHOSPITABLE TERRAIN: The Sahara Desert writes its memoirs

IRRATION IN THE NATION: after Reggae is officially adopted as the national music of Great Britain – the Chancellor of the Exchequer unwisely decides to speak street in a daily Mail interview describing the mood of the people after he has put up taxes on everything for the millionth time

ITALIAN OPERA APPRECIATION SOCIETY And DOMESTIC REMOVALS: New Jersey Branch of The Sopranos

IT'S NOT UNUSUAL: when asked if he still likes to wear panties thrown at him on stage in the 1960s, the famous Welsh singer cannot resist a nostalgic reply

IVOR BIGGUN: Ivor Smallpiece tries new chat up line to get girls

JOHNNY ON THE JOB

JACKASS: in a rare tell-all interview, Jill puts the record straight in the Brothers Grimm edition of Cosmopolitan about what first attracted her to Jack on the hill (and it wasn't water)

JAILHOUSE ROCK: sticks of candy available in the Wormwood Scrubs Prison Gift Shop

JAGGED EDGE: U2's guitar player sharpens cutlery in his Dublin kitchen

JAMES LAST: James The First's dumber brother

JAWBREAKING SIGHT: girlfriend watches her Boxing Fiancé dole out physical medicine to former a former lothario boyfriend of hers

JOHN THOMAS: An upper-class penis - Reginald Bosenquet Thomas IV - takes a more ordinary name to avoid jibes: Elton John gives his favourite appendage a nickname

JOHNNIE B. GOODE: fridge magnet in Johnny Depp's bedroom at the Betty Ford Clinic for Sexual Addiction

JOHNNY CASH: legendary country singer refuses royalty payments by PayPal

JOHNNY ON THE JOB: a sensitivity tester in a Durex Factory

JOINT STATEMENT: a huge rack of Roast Beef tells an enrapt audience of lonely vegetarians what it's like to be in an oven for hours on end with Bisto and Onions as your only friends

JPEG: clothes attachment on Jennifer Lopez's washing line

JUPITER RISING: after seeing Venus undress, a big planet has a big erection

JUST DESERTS: In yet another brilliant diversity equity inclusivity move, the Sahara and Gobi Deserts are nominated as two non-binary High Court Justices in a Democrats Party Convention in Vegas

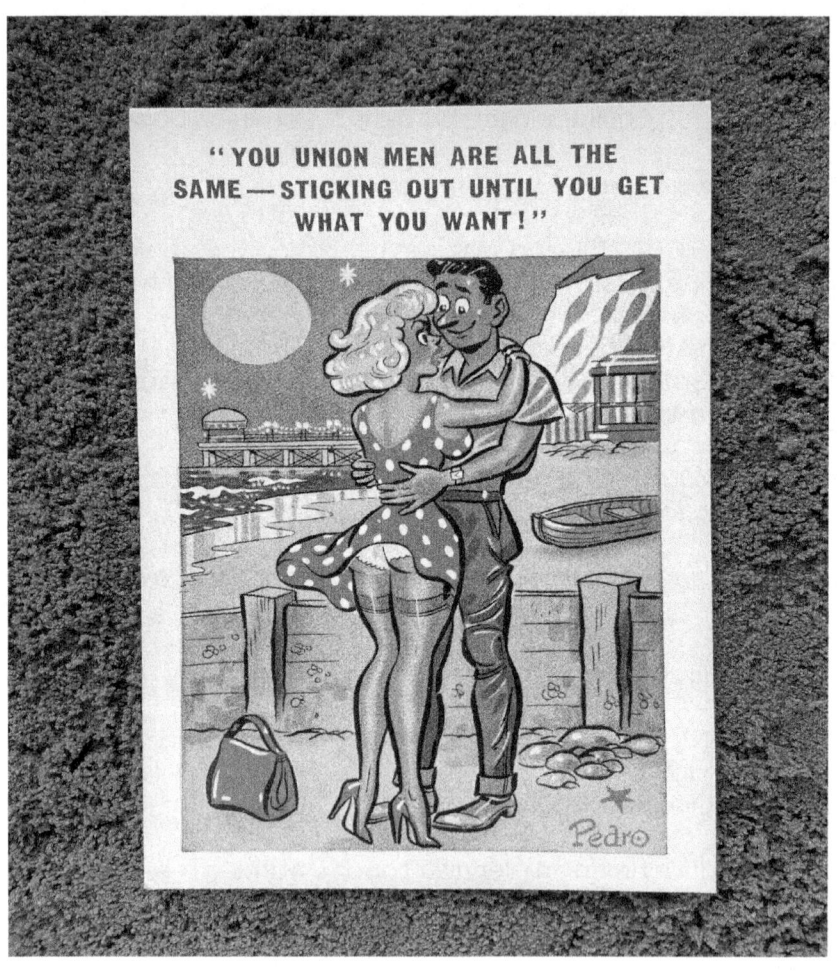

KNICKERBOCKER GLORY

KEEN AS MUSTARD: Irish Football Legend *Roy Keane* camouflages his erection in the presence Miss Melons 2025 with a large jar of Colman's

KEYSTONE COPS: police arrest a suspicious looking concrete brick lingering outside a locksmith's home

KICKBOXER: a pair of M&S men's shorts gets a Black Belt at Taekwondo

KING KONG: largish Gorilla admires his undercarriage during a relaxing holiday break in New York

KINKY BOOTS: A British high street chemist chain sells sex toys, strawberry flavoured dildos and Nutella-flavoured bondage equipment in a bid to increase sales and customer footfall

KNEADING DOUGH: a bankrobber makes a not-unexpected request of his local Nat West Manager

KNICKERBOCKER GLORY: a high-kicking chorus-line of Can Can girls in Paris's Moulin Rouge finally decide to shed their frilly pantalets altogether and show their dancehall punters the true wonders of French au natural

KNICKERS: Hampstead Ladies who steal underwear in Marks & Spencer Oxford Street to avoid local shame; saucier relative of an American Candy Bar with chocolate and nuts that's dropped the first letter of its name in a defiant street cred move

KNOB GAG: Harvey Weinstein looks forward to many hours of silence during his forth-coming prison sentence

KNOWLEDGE: a pigeon asks for directions to the nearest open window

(A COUPLE OF) KOOKS: two Gourmet chefs with surnames that end in K open a new restaurant in Soho

LICKITY SPLIT

A LABOUR OF LOVE: British political party gets all touchy-feely: Mrs. Stalin describes giving birth to her latest working son as her husband stands nearby with a direct line to the Gulag

LASER PRINTER: after he finds out the extortionate prices of replacement cartridges, Obi-wan Kenobi has a Jedi hissy fit and accidentally uses the dark side of the force to light-sabre his admittedly budget-range Brother Inkjet

LAY LADY LAY: Chinese Government Officials mistakes its female population for chickens: Chinese Government Officials try to coax Chinese women into having more than one baby by playing them a well-known American song over loudspeakers

LEAD SINGER: very heavy sewing machine

LEG ROOM: 22 fashion models in a lift [see also DIZZY HEIGHTS]

LEMON DRIZZLE: April shower gets through the roof of Mr. Kipling's exceedingly good cake factory

LETTUCE BOWL: tee-shirt worn by Jeff Bridge's *Dude* character in The Big Lebowski; wanting to get away from prodding hands, a depressed garden vegetable seeks permission to leave his Pizza Hut Salad Bar tray to go play his favourite indoor 10-pin ball-game

LIBIDO: an outdoor swimming pool in Hugh Hefner's Playboy Mansion

LICKITY SPLIT: porn actress demonstrates on a Solero ice-cream how to get a get a quick (pay) rise from your boss

LIE BACK AND THINK OF ENGLAND: British housewife finds her husband's lovemaking so slow that she has time to think about Ireland, Scotland and Wales too during the process

LIGHT-HEARTED HUMOUR: underweight Aorta shares a joke with his surgeon

LOADSTAR: Hollywood type informs his unsuspecting date of incoming

LOCALISE: a pair of sunglasses seeks retinas that live near nearby

LONDON MARRIOTT HOTEL: regular haunt for cheeky-chappy Lead Singer with The Small Faces and Humble Pie

THE LONG AND SHORT OF IT: a giraffe and a titmouse discuss vagina-targeting strategies

LONG JOHN SILVER: taking his first hot-water bath in six months, a gold-rush prospector is disappointed to find a cheaper kind of metal fall out of his filthy underwear

LOONEY TUNES: in-house Radio Station in an insane asylum

LOSE FIVE POUNDS: lady of the night explains to a circuit judge of the exact nocturnal monetary loses she will incur for five minutes down time due to temporary incarceration (your honour)

LOVE TRAIN: The American Soul group The O'Jays renames the Friday night 5:20pm *Kiss-Me-Quick* Weekend Away Train Special to Blackpool

LUBRICANT: suppository claims it can no longer do its job

LUGGAGE: a very old ear refuses to admit its age at Airport Security

LUKE FARTYPANTS: (kept at a) Distant Cousin of Luke Skywalker

LUKE PEEWALKER: Elderly Uncle of Luke Skywalker

LUXURY HAND WASH: complimentary after-service offered to regulars at Lusty Lil's Night Club in Las Vegas

MUTINY ON THE BOUNTY

MADAM SPEAKER: female political orator; porn star voice used on an X-Rated version of The Teletubbies (see also MISTER SPEAKER)

MADAME SIN: mistress of Beelzebub; French Lady takes a surname more descriptive of her physical needs

MAGNUM OPUS: Wall's Icecream Lolly now only identifies as a Beethoven Concerto

MAIDENHEAD: to promote more footfall and gain extra revenue, a local barmaid in a Berkshire town is inundated with male customers when she says she'll pull them a free stiff one with every bag of crisps purchased

MAKE UP THE NUMBERS: Joe Biden sits in on a Mensa meeting and is asked about DOGE discoveries (Department of Government Efficiency) in the Democratic Party for Four Years of Public Expenditure Waste, but his wife and cocaine-addled son Hunter Biden both give a cryptic reply

MAMA TOLD ME NOT TO COME: during a divorce case, an Irish Catholic husband admits in court that at the crucial moment, he never satisfied his ex-Protestant wife in 24 years of marriage because of parental advice from his beloved mother

THE MAN FROM U.N.C.L.E.: A 1960s Napoleon Solo type secret agent avoiding Jilly Ridesemall THE WOMAN WITH T.H.R.U.S.H.

MANDATE: password used with the bouncers at the doors of The Communards Reunion After Hours Party in Old Compton Street

MARRIAGE COUNCELLOR: Irish barman at the Dog and Duck in Camden Town

MARS BAR: unimaginatively-named first pub on the Red Planet

MARS BARS: a notorious set of saloons in the Red District on the Red Planet

MATCHING PAIR: Porn star describes her most popular attributes

MEET CUTE: Two Pork Chops admire each other; A Sirloin Steak and a Doner Kebab go on a first date

MELLOW YELLOW: a Dandelion tokes on a spliff for the first time

MESSAGE IN A BOTTLE: marooned on a Tropical island with sex-starved Polynesian nubiles, former Police front man leaves note in Olive Oil bottle for his ex-girlfriend Roxanne stating that she can turn off the red light

MIDDLESEX: not-so-bright husband-and-wife-duo are informed that he should have been poking his wife's vagina these last 25 years and not her navel

MIKE HUNT: unfortunate name of Mrs. Hunt's husband

MILK TRAY: Marks and Spencer's behind the counter waitress Samantha with 38GGG chest offers her left breast to customers on a canteen platter as an entre

MIND'S EYE: Casanova wonders does the tip of his penis have either a brain or a conscience

MING DYNASTY: Transgender Rock Band goes shopping for delph; in stilettos and wigs planning Global Domination beginning next Wednesday

MING VASE: Chinese Woman concerned about extremely pungent five-thousand-year-old dragon jism odours emanating from a dirt-cheap ceramic kiln in her Beijing outhouse/latrine

MISSIONARY POSITION: a convent of nuns in Maidenhead, loosen their vow of chastity and allow one angle of physical pleasure (and only then, if you're thinking of England)

MISTER SPEAKER: male political orator; particularly macho Bang & Olufsen stereo

MISTLETOE AND WINE: a drunk vicar stubs his digit at a Xmas Party

MIXED METAPHORE: Overly excited by a recent punctuation discovery, a White Noun sleeps with a Black Adjective at a KKK Verbal Abuse and Dictionary Appreciation Rally (nine months later they call their child Meet Cute)

MOANING MYRTLE: Welsh husband welcomes his wife's vocal responses during anal sex

MOBSTER: Tony Soprano's sports car

MOCKINGBIRD: Girl Parrot chastises her Budgie boyfriend's lack of Thrill in his tray

MODUS OPERANDI: modus conveniently located beside a 1970s Space Hopper

MOMENTUM: a confused moment

MONO: Bono's nickname for his mum (see also STEREO)

MOTT THE HOOPLE: Hula Hoops becomes the staple diet for "All The Young Dudes" band

MOUSE GLUE TRAP: Security measure used at Disneyland if Mickey Mouse does Cocaine again

MOUSE ON A MOTORCYCLE: a bike courier passes wind on his Honda 50

MUSTANG SALLY: lovechild of Pink Cadillac and Little Red Corvette; distant relative of Coup DeVille and second cousin removed of Mohair Sam

MUTINY ON THE BOUNTY: ship's crew strike over lack of well-known chocolate and cocoanut bars on the dinner menu

MY DING-A-LING: Chuck Berry sings proudly of his *musical longevity*

MYOCARDITUS: gambler admits an inexplicable passion for the 0 on a 10 card

No BONES ABOUT IT

NAVAL CADET: a young bellybutton

NEARBY: two bisexuals standing beside each other

NEAT AND TIDY: Casanova reveals his two-prong genitalia grooming strategy to get girls

NECK BRACE: a point somewhere between a Pint of Smithwicks and a Hickey

NEEDFUL THINGS: a Sourdough Shop that sells only huge loaves; a ladies club states their willy-wedge preference

NERD: a teenage Maths student with Albert Einstein's photo as his profile image, has twice the IQ but unfortunately none of the charm; possibly owns the world and everything else for that matter

NIBLOCK: a safe in the home of a fountain pen

NO BONES ABOUT IT: recently re-animated 1719 Georgian Skeleton admits real reason for failure of his first blind date with a woman in nearly three hundred years

NO NAY NEVER: name of the building that houses AA Headquarters

NOBIWOOD: Pinocchio name's his penis

NODULES: sign outside the Three Musketeers favourite bordello

NUBILE: a sick-bag prepares for fresh incoming

NUGGETS: a 1967 Psych Band from California called NUG scores magic mushrooms on the hippie trail in Goa

NUMPTY: Humpty Dumpty's suspect brother

NUTTERY: hand-painted sign on the wall of the men's loo pointing back to the debating chambers in The House of Commons

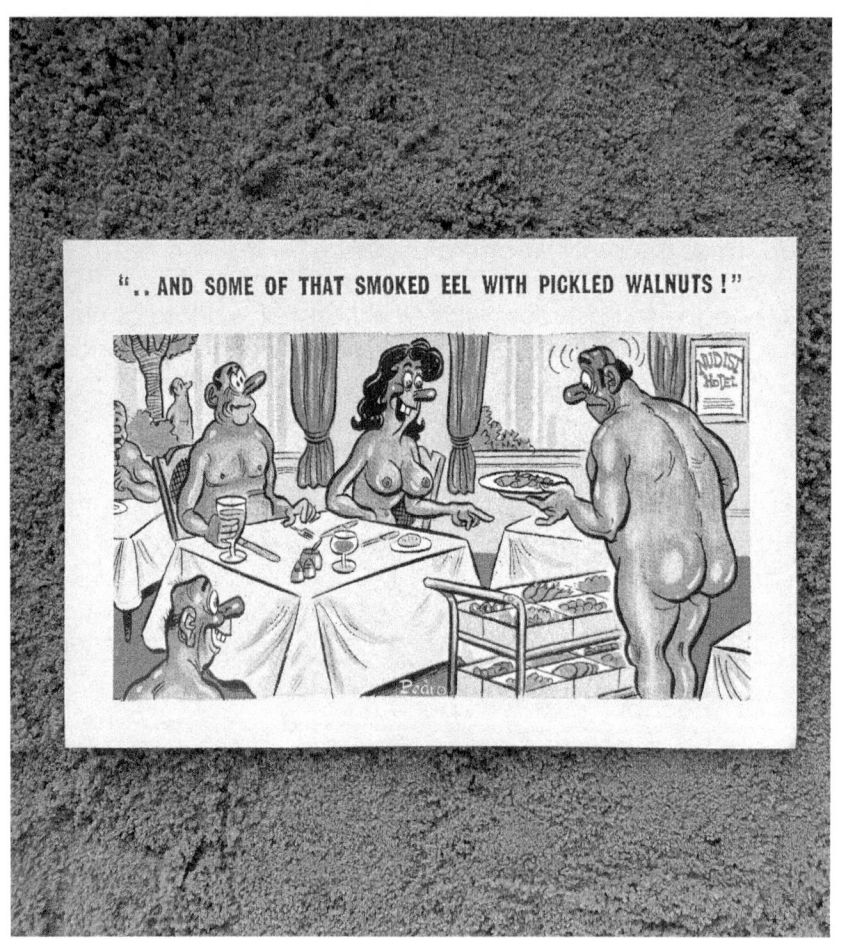

ORIGINAL SIN

OCTOPUSSY: a Working Girl visits The House Of Commons eight times during recess: 007 James Bond actor Sir Roger Moore reminisces on the number of ladies he had to sleep with on Bond

OFFENSIVE FULLBACK: American Football player describes his annoyance at the size of his opponents rear charger

OFFSIDE RULE: football club that only allows perpendicular lovemaking during showers

OILY RAG: Fish and Chips wrapped in a Daily Mail and/or The Sun

OMG: nickname of Olly Mur's sports car

ON TERRA FIRMA: In a candid interview about the legendary Monty Python actor, writer and film maker, Terry Gilliam's wife describes her husband's first erection

OPEN HOUSE: High on Adderall, Hugh Laurie bends over and takes one for the medical team

ORAL WARNING: rule in a Blowjob Competition

ORANGE PEEL: President Donald Trump stops into a Florida beauty salon for a facial

ORANGUTAN: hotline to a tanning salon

ORCHESTRATION: wind-section in a Bra-making factory

ORDERED IN FOR THE NIGHT: Casanova tells his John Thomas to give it a rest

ORGAN DONOR: Casanova then baulks at latest body-part donation request from the Italian Medical Institute to further science

ORGAN RECITAL: Casanova placates the Italian Medical Academy by sending them a song his famous pecker made up just for them

ORIGINAL SIN: first man *Adam* wears the wrong foliage on his debut date with *Eve*

OSCAR WILDE: perpetual slob in The Odd Couple (Oscar Madison) finally loses it and picks up a napkin to please his tidiness flatmate Felix Unger, but it only annoys Felix even more because Oscar doesn't fold it

OSCILLOSCOPE: a device that measures Cilla Black's orgasms

OSTRACIZE: a machine that measures the length of Ostrich penises

THE OTHER WOMAN: Corporate Boss ignores his busty secretary and falls in love instead with the undercarriage of a Friesian Heifer

OTHERWORLDLY FEELING: Site Manager on a Jupiter Moon mining facility touches up his robot secretary in a moment of lurid weakness

OTTOMAN EMPIRE: Turkish ruler renames every male in his domain after himself

OUR LADY OF PERPETUAL SORROW: British Prime Minister Theresa May during two years of Brexit negotiations

OUNCE OF PASSION: titmouse tells his love that what he lacks in size and coital heft, he more than makes up for in application

OUT OF SIGHT, OUT OF MIND: alas, poor Yorick's skull realises that its missing several key components to a happy life

OUTER SPACE: British Prime Minister Boris Johnson comes up with a far-reaching solution for the UK housing crisis

OUTSTANDING IN HIS OWN FIELD: farmer enjoys the aroma of newly turned soil in his own pasture; cow-dung expert steps into his favourite tipple

PLANTING THE PARSNIP

PAIN IN THE ASS: singer Barry Manilow describes coming out in his new tell-all autobiography "Mandy Came And Gave Without Taking"

PANIC STATIONS: F.M. Radio Bands that only play EMO Music, 24-7; F.M. Radio Band for *End Of The World* enthusiasts

PANTALOONS: out-of-breath patients from "One Flew Over The Cuckoo's Nest" take a breather with Nurse Ratched after their daily jog to the pill dispensary

PAPA WAS A ROLLING STONE: a button on the teeshirt of Bill Wyman's daughter

PAPYRUS: Pyrex Casserole Dish found in ancient Egyptian tomb with receipt attached and copyright name spelt incorrectly

PARAZONE: an Irish Army *Boy Band* tribute act

PARDON MY FRENCH: Bridgette Macron apologises to foreign dignitaries for her overly macho kiss-greetings

PARIS HILTON: American Celebrity at the reception of a famous Parisienne Hotel suggests a name change

PAY DIRT: one square inch of soil in London

PEACHWOOD: scientists find a direct correlation between a woman's figure and its effect on the male member

PEAK PERFORMANCE: married couple fulfil a lifelong ambition to shag on the summit of Mount Everest while commercial airliners go by

PEARLY GATES: St. Peter gets in touch with his feminine side and decorates the entrance to Heaven with girly apparel (see also CRIMINAL PARTS)

PECKERHEAD: Leaving the lab, Dr. Frankenstein's Creature discovers that his maker has placed his bit-part willy in an awkward place

PEDIGREE CHUM: a friendly Chihuahua mounts a stool in a stable and offers a thoroughbred racehorse some of his lunch; an emotional Show Dog winner cries in front of a tearful panel of judges as he strokes his 1st Place Rosette, citing his Parisian trainer Marcel as his biggest inspiration and pal

PENCIL PUSHER: a wife describes her husband's lovemaking technique to a marriage councillor; a bully in a Geometry Box

PERPETUAL MOTION: once purring house cat now stuck on its owners walking exercise machine that won't switch off

PIG IN A POKE: Ghislaine Maxwell, socialite and wife of disgraced sexual predator and abuser Jeffrey Epstein, is found hiding in an upstate New York pig sty stroking a picture of someone's teenage daughter

PIGGY BANK: swine behind the loan's counter in Nat West Croydon Branch

PISS 'N' VINEGAR: condiments in a Margate Fish 'n' Chips shop

PISTOLS AT DAWN: British Punk Rock Group wakes up naked in Dawn French's living room

PIZZA EXPRESS: Well-known alibi-haunt for high society underage sex traffickers

PLANTING THE PARSNIP: Gertrude Wonderheave, the buxom Bavarian labourer, discovers that a local farmer's claim to want to plant seeds in her rills has little to do with Horticulture

POACHER: adamant anti-hardboiled activist, a Farm Thief is particular about how he has his two stolen eggs in the morning

POLE POSITION: Casanova advises his latest artistic muse where to sit

POLISHED FINISH: a Helsinki Diplomat admires his expertly dusted pippeli

POLITICAL CORRECTNESS: rather than deal with the real issues, a tactic used by British politicians to point the finger of blame at someone else whilst looking like they care; watered down words for politicians who haven't the guts to tell the naysayers to fuck right off and die - and they don't have the decency to do either – fuck right off or die; a way of the media stifling descent; false outrage publicly displayed to allow politicians a way to look like they care but actually have no moral centre of any kind while they shaft the poor, the broken, the dispossessed and those areas of society that are least able to defend themselves – the elderly, the poor, special needs, women's issues; a lie pretending to be concern even outrage

POONANNY: An elderly Aunt who can't get to the toilet as fast as she used to; part of a woman that excites men silly but bores gynaecologists shitless

POSITIVE THINKING: Having a dump whilst reading Marie Kondo's new best seller *How To Unclutter Smaller Spaces*

POTTY TRAINING: insane asylum resident claims that the pill-popping, drooling and electro-shock therapy regime of his former life prepared him fully for his new role as a member of the UKIP Party; infants watch YouTube videos on how to make your family even more insane in the future than they already are

POUND FOR POUND: Madam Susie Sidepiece offers her services to a sentencing judge for a very reasonable fee in lieu of a jail sentence

POWER TO THE PEOPLE: John Lennon tries to woo back customers to Southern Electricity after massive power outage during a vigorous bed-in

PRAISEWORTHY: Worthington Ale rep explains to rookie how to get on

PREGNANT PAUSE: a family cat in a family way takes a load off

PRIG: a pretentious twig; a dyslexic hairpiece

PRIME TIME: Happy hour for ZZ Top at the Big Texan Steak House

PRO BONO: the name of the legal team in Cher's first divorce; John McEnroe commenting on the Wimbledon tennis skills of U2's lead singer

PRODUCING EUPHORIC EFFECTS: Drug-Binge At an Industrial Light and Magic Star Wars board meeting

PROPOGANDA: Uganda's Ministry for Misinformation

PRUNE PUNCH: a Boxing Match in a Retirement Home

PUB CRAWL: Peter O'Toole and Oliver Reed try to get to the boozer exit door after a night on the raz

PUBERTY: phone-app taxi service for teens

PUBESCENT: fizzy drink made from scrotum hair (all ages)

PULLMAN SEATS: section on The Orient Express reserved for Gay Men

PUPPY LOVE: Seventies heartthrob Donny Osmond expresses worrying interest in canines (instead of girls) to the reader's page of Jackie

PURE BREED: name on the white sheet of the Ku Klux Klan's lead horse carrying Betty Sue Chastity White in the 1953 Miss Mississippi Beauty Pageant; name of the racehorse entered by the British National Front in The Aintree Races

PUSHING UP DAISIES: Daisy the Milkmaid tries a new cleavage-enhancing bra

PUSSYFOOTING AROUND: Dr. Martens launch a new boot range for women with the promise that it will provide more stimulation than just a feeling of walking on air

PUSSY GALORE: message left on the answering machine at Hugh Heffner's Playboy Mansion; best-dressed flight instructor ever

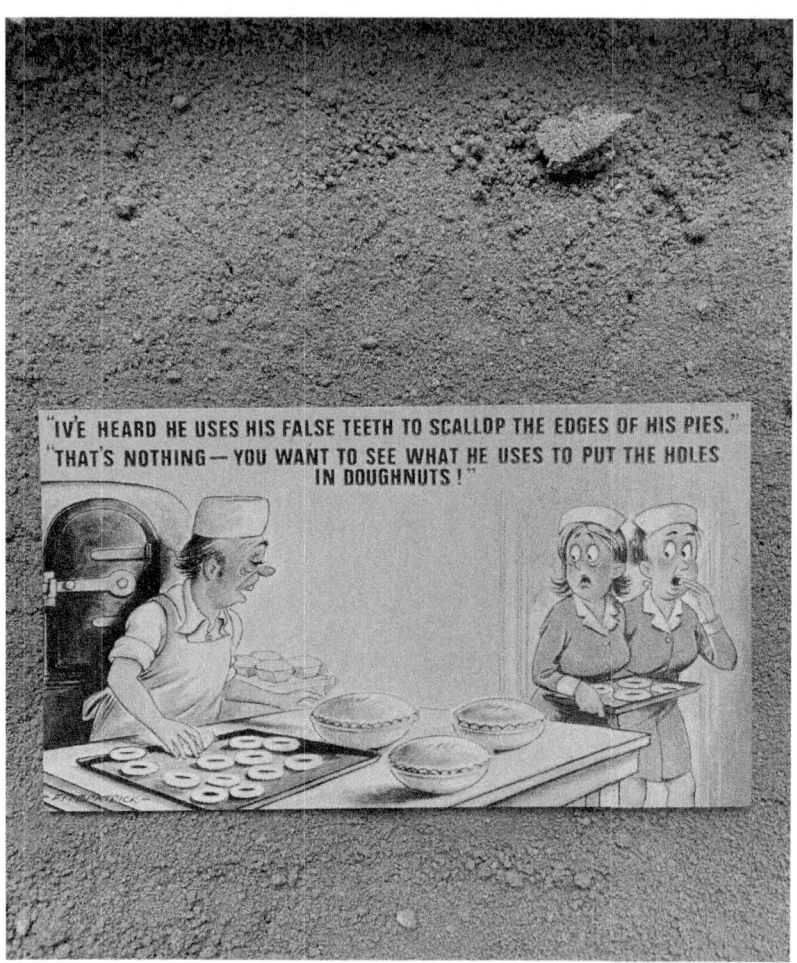

QUICK SHUFTY

QUACK REMEDIES: a Doctor gives his expert opinion on Daffy Duck's chilblains

QUALITY TIME: a Rolex likes what he sees in the mirror

QUADRUPLE BYPASS: Russian Heart Surgeon finds a bunch of coins in his patient's chest cavity

QUANTUM LEAP: an iPad takes up pole-vaulting

QUARTERLY ACCOUNTS: a misgendered number 4 speaks its mind on Breakfast TV

QUASHED: a bottle of Dilute Orange has a parking ticket supressed

QUEASY: a passenger of an Easy Jet holiday falls ill

QUESTIONABLE: Kane askes his brother about the plot in a Jeffrey Archer novel

QUESTIONABLE METHODS: an Earthling asks his Alien Captor if the Anal Probe is completely necessary

A QUICK SHUFTY: biological need carried out in car parks, fields, forests, brush patches, cinemas, airplane toilets, back seats of Volkswagens and other locations of carnal interest during the first year of courtship (the following 25 years of said courtship are noticeable by the complete absence of the shufties)

QUIT THE DAY JOB: a reminder about humility *Post It* note on God's refrigerator regarding control over his expanding Universe

QUITE HARD: Lady of the Night generously describes her punter's drunken ardour

QUITTER: mans decides not to poop in local toilets

RUMPY PUMPY

RABBLE ROUSER: practising her routines, a Campus Cheerleader moves a male student protest march to bigger things

RAINING CATS AND DOGS: Hurricane Katrina passes over London's Battersea Dogs and Cats Home

RASPBERRY RIPPLE: a headlight visible through Delia Smith's lacy bra on BBC 1's "Bake Off"; Delia Smith's bra has a wardrobe moment on Celebrity Chef

REBUTTAL: American defence lawyer once again says the accused has a massive bottom: Sumo Wrestler offers tips to newcomers on how to recycle undercarriage nappies

RECORD COLLECTORS: a prison entirely filled with vinyl thieves

RECREATIONAL SEX: suburban couple combine wallpapering the kitchen with the missionary position to coordinate paste strokes

RECTUM: Doctor answers a question on the outcome to his patient's latest anal procedure with a light-hearted rebuttal – "Rectum? It nearly killed him!"

THE RED CARPET: the nickname given to Harvey Weinstein's rug in his Virginal Actress Auditions Suite

THE RED PLANET: American manned mission to Mars is horrified to find that Russians have colonised it decades back and the red world in now in fact peopled by the largest number of floating Communists anywhere in the Universe

RED RUM: Communist spy working at Langley Headquarters craftily disguised as a drunken racehorse

REGIONAL DISH: cardboard cut-out of English model Kelly Brook is used to entice customers into a Birmingham branch of Sky

REVENGE IS SWEET: irate wife who stabs her husband in the eye again treats herself to a Jam Roly Poly after the event

REVISIONIST: University Chemistry Professor awards an A instead of a C to a female student on loan from the Baywatch set after her fantastic paper on *How To Make His Erlenmeyer Boil*

ROBIN: drop-in facility in Haringey for thieves of all races, colours and creeds; self-awareness course for burglars (see also BATMAN)

ROCK ARCHIVES: a history of black porn stars and their unfeasible huge phalluses (see HARD ROCK CAFÉ)

ROCK OUT WITH YOUR COCK OUT: Iggy Pop feels that showing his naked torso on stage no longer goes far enough and therefore bears his favourite appendage for Rock 'n' Roll; the mental mantra of every frontman whose every been in a band

ROOT CANAL: vegetarian dentist chews a delicious organically grown celery stick during molar extraction

ROSE BUSH: on their honeymoon in Las Vegas, Korean pole dancer 'Pussy Flower' opens her legs and shows her new mail-order Texas horticulturalist husband Bob Crotchangeau where he needs to get gardening on their first night together

ROUGH DAY AT THE OFFICE: on the last Friday of every month, the men must wear only industrial strength sandpaper as clothing

ROUGH DIAMOND: nightclub bouncer working in a Hatton Garden jewellery shop; bulldog whose swallowed Liz Taylor's eighth engagement ring

RUINATION: the Dustbowl town of Ruin fires its hopeless Tourist Board after abysmal visitor figures

RUNE STONES: the worst vocalist in the word replaces Mick Jagger as Lead Singer of The Rolling Stones leading to the legendary band's downfall

(THE) RUMPY PUMPY: a Dildo in the Arnold Schwarzenegger gift shop

SHOTGUN WEDDING

SACRED BOND: British Agent 007 points to his crown jewels during a routine field-readiness physical

SAFE AND SOUND: dynamite-using burglar describes his two favourite things about his local jewellers

SAILOR'S HORNPIPE: Captain Hook secretly lusts after Tinkerbell

SALE OF THE CENTURY: the years 1901 to 1999 are offered on EBAY with a starting price of one hundred pounds

SALT CELLAR: man offering bargain bottles of Saxa in Sainsbury's Food Hall

SANTA CLAUS: a knackered Kris Kringle realises there's no way out of reindeer shit-shovelling duty following a very busy Christmas

SAUCES AND DRIZZLES: a troupe of Pole-Dancers visits a premature ejaculation conference

SAVED HIS BACON: To an enrapt audience at the annual Ladies Meat Packers Christmas Party, Mrs. Porky Pig regales a story of how she once rescued her husband from a marauding bunch of ravenous builders rummaging for a butty breakfast in the staff canteen

SCHOLARSHIP: Harvard Mathematics Professor on a Caribbean cruise

SCRAWL TO THE WALL: Banksy's Autobiography

SEAFOOD CRABS: diver gets a STD from sleeping too much with a morally dubious crustacean

SEARCH ENGINE: the motor inside the new 2025 Tesla Model 2 is so advanced, it can find slippers behind the couch and parking tickets from 1967

SECONDRY DIAGONAL: a cheerleaders notices that *two* football jocks may be interested in more than her poms-poms

SELF CONFESSED SERIAL ABUSER: US Evangelist admits addiction to Kellogg's Cornflakes

SELF RAISING FLOUR: a meadow dandelion mistakenly thinks it's a porn star and attempts an erection for a comely and voluptuous nearby daisy

SEMEN COUNT: name of Monica Lewinski's autobiography; submariners tally up ejaculation stains on their bunk-bed sheets after six months in the Baring Straights

SEMI CONDUCTOR: part time leader of the London Symphony Orchestra; Leader of the LSO who can't detach himself from his Orchestra

SENIOR MANAGEMENT: ex Sicilian Mafia Boss controls the Pill Trolley at a Florida Retirement Home

SERIAL OFFENDERS: Dr. John Kellogg prescribes a bowl of his cornflakes every evening to the boys in his clinic as a cure for excessive teenage masturbation, but instead finds they like it too much and want more

SEVERAL WEEKS: a group of puny men sign up to a bodybuilding course for a fortnight

SEXUAL ARROUSAL: Melanie Trump seeks therapy after strange sensation in her marriage

SHAKESPEARE: Advice sign outside a urinal for Zulu Warriors

SHETLAND PONY: slang for a freshly minted dump on a certain Scottish Island

SHIT HAPPENS: title given to an art installation at the Tate Modern where today's Times newspaper is smeared with several mounds of the artist's excrement and mounted on a gargantuan white wall (the newspaper is freshly minted each day of the exhibition)

SHIVER ME TIMBERS: Sycamore Tree holidays in an Igloo

SHOTGUN WEDDING: broke fiancé Lolita Von Tramp marries wealthy sheriff Wyatt Earp in the OK Corral Chapel at 10:45 a.m. due to impending shootout in the streets at 10:55 a.m.

SILENT BUT DEADLY: a First Officer farts in a US nuclear submarine that's gone dark beneath the Russian ice (no one says anything)

SINGLE FILE: contacts for ladies in James Bond's Rolodex

SINGER SONGWRITER: Elton John at a sewing machine

SIX-SPEED GEARBOX: Formula One Racing Driver describes sexual intercourse with a Rubik's Cube

SKELETON CREW: passengers on a Ryanair flight from Dublin to Lourdes are alarmed to find that the cabin crew have taken their company's less-weight-is-good mantra a little too far by not eating for an entire year

SKYWALKER: young Tatooine farm boy takes a sleep-deprived but deeply unwise stroll on the speeding flaps of an X-Wing

SLAP AND TICKLE: corporal punishment office finds his wife in bed with a feather duster

SLIM PICKINGS: anorexic model stoops in field to gather strawberries for Royal Ascot; even skinner model at a South Wales coalface with an axe in hand;

SLUG: a bullet in no hurry

SLUG AND LETTUCE: a Snail and Iceberg Leaf find love on Tinder

SLURRING HIS LINES: drunken worker resurfacing the M25 in the early hours of the morning goes off course on his paint-dispensing tractor; an actor portraying the notorious Hellraiser Oliver Reed goes a little too method with a bottle of vino on the Graham Norton Show

SMOKING POT: Pol Pot's sexy Cambodian sister Kylie Mare Rouge (see also FRUITY POTS); chimney stack admits inhaling after years claiming it was just puffing; London Fire Brigade called to out to Kew Gardens to douse a blazing terracotta holder full of pyromaniacal Geraniums

SNICKERS BAR: a Pub in the Bronx that only serves candy treats with a condescending snigger

SNOOZE BUTTON: what Mrs. Rip Van Winkle's wife reaches for when her husband wants sex

SNOW WHITE: Ku Klux Klan meeting in the town of Ingrate, Tennessee unfortunately cancelled due to adverse weather conditions outside Chuck Goodguy's "Niggers R Us" Steak House: nickname for the outer casing of Hunter Biden's laptop

SOAP DISPENSERS: Coronation Sheet flavoured Durex dispenser

SOAP OPERA: Puccini's lost masterpiece about an Italian Count's forbidden love affair with a bar of Cousin's Imperial Leather

SOCK DRAWER: a pair of Clark's shoes finds that it's a sexual magnet for Marks and Spenser's 100% cotton footsies; an Avant Garde French artist who only paints multipacks of ankle socks

SOMETHING INSIDE SO STRONG: Singer Labi Siffre wakes up from a nightmare only to find that in his leading role as Nancy the Gay Wrestler of Downtown California, Arnold Schwarzenegger has taken method acting too far and is trying to mount him

SPANDEX: a Jane Fonda exercise workout video from 1986 goes on a 40th Anniversary *cruise* in 2026: a gym for former members of Spandau Ballet

SPEED BUMPS: Two heavily pregnant women racing through the doors of a Maternity Hospital at the same time

SPEED DATING: a way to fully appreciate the recently oiled hinges of nearby swinging doors; a tactless but economical way to acquire a nutritional evening meal while JackFromBognor1958 pays for it; Keanu Reeves and Lewis Hamilton share notes on fast women

SPIRITS IN THE MATERIAL WORLD: Glenfiddich Whiskey Bottles found in a Dundee kilt factory; ghosts of former Prime Ministers who haunt the late-night corridors of 10 Downing Street

SPORTS ILLUSTRATED: Van Gogh's long-lost painting masterpiece of an ear-slicing competition set against a backdrop of Dutch Sunflowers

SPRING SALE: used mattress-supports going cheap on eBay

STAIN REMOVAL: Monica Lewinsky describes to a Grand Jury the nature of President Clinton's campaign contributions

STAPLE DIET: an office paper-punch considers a new ingredient in its ongoing quest for weight-loss

STEREO: U2's nickname for The Edge's testicles (see also MONO)

STARK NAKED: Iron Man (character's name is Tony Stark) in a Nudist Camp

STRAIGHT SHOOTER: a marksman in the Gay Olympics is disqualified when it's found out that he lied and has had a longtime girlfriend

STRAITJACKET: British Fashion Police issue new uniforms for writers at Vogue

STRICTLY COME DANCING: male bondage stripper in Solihull gets carried away during the climax of his Dungeons & Dragons dance routine

STUD FARM: a ranch full of riveters; Yellowstone Gift Shop for the ladies

SUBCATEGORY: Captain Nemo's autobiography

SUBVERSIVE BEHAVIOUR: a Poet on the Nautilus acts strange

SUCCEEDS: a gummy budgie

SUCCUBUS: conductor blows his own double-decker's tailpipe

SUCKED DOWN UNDER: A British Gay Man explains why he emigrated to Australia

SUDDEN MOVES: a Bottle of Fairy Liquid gets an erection

SUGARCOATED: Blowjob Champion of the World admits her favourite tipple

SUNKEN GARDENS: Alan Titchmarsh discovers evidence of Azalea pruning in Atlantis

SUNNY SIDE OF THE STREET: North Korean President Kim Jong-un describes the joy and illumination he felt at seeing his country's first nuclear weapon tested a few blocks away

SUPER BOWL: The Man of Steel's cereal dish

SWANKY RESTAURANT: high-end Soho eatery that encourages masturbation between courses

SWAYING IN THE WIND: Ballroom Dancing instructor couple bravely continue their Waltz during an outbreak of farting from the other elderly contestants

SWEAR BOX: A TV made in Ireland

SWEATPANTS: Casanova gives a nickname to his Pantaloons

SWEEPSTAKES: steak night at a road-sweepers house

SWEEPING STATEMENT: a flood of tears vows to alter its whingy ways

SWELTERING CONDITIONS: rule-list posted outside a sauna

SWINGING DOORS: see SPEED DATING

SWINGING SIXTIES: British pensioners meeting in forests to exchange each other; during a bra-burning ritual in Hyde Park, British feminists let their natural talents sway in the sunshine

SWOOPED DOWN: a Falcon gets the Blues

TOP PRIORITY

TAKE A HIKE: Gift Voucher at Yosemite National Park

TAKING FLACK: Sun Newspaper Editor steals better-worded insults from The Times Editor during drunken Fleet Street lunch

TALISMAN: small-chested Latvian Pole Dancer Tal receives disturbing news from a DNA paternity test

TALKING DOG: precocious Siamese cat retracts her emotional trauma claim of not having enough Jimmy Chu shoes to wee and shit in and instead describes to an enrapt jury and courtroom the real reason why she left former owner's home

TARGET ON HIS HEAD: Donald Trump smiles as he crayons a Bullseye on a Mexican child's forehead

TEA TOTAL: In between Futterwacken dances, Mad Hatter (of Alice In Wonderland) counts the number of PG Tips he's had at parties

TEARS OF A CLOWN: As dictator Kim Jong-un has another tantrum and launches its first nuclear missile at the American mainland despite his treaty with the U.S.A., President Donald Trump hears the bad news on the white house phone while at the same realising that he's left the case and the keys to the nuclear launch-codes in a gym locker (he'd been working out with Miss Teen Texas as boys do)

TEMPUS FUGIT: A Rolex on Concorde: a Roman airline for Gladiators in a hurry

THERE SHE BLOWS: Admiral Nelson suspects *more* than a fair-wind is working his column

THREE WISE MEN: scientists discover that the number of coherent politicians in the world is alarmingly lower than they had first thought

THICK AS THIEVES: rejected Mensa applications rob a bank

TIT FOR TAT: in a frenzy of seasonal environmentalism at Christmas, a woman has an image of a garbage bag tattooed on her left breast in protest: a Hooker offers a part of her anatomy for a bargain find at a garage sale

TOAD IN THE HOLE: Roger Ailes, notoriously handsy head of Fox News USA, is found with his penis stuck in a specially carved-out cavity under his desk (see also PIG IN A POKE)

TONGUE-TIED: Speaker of The House Of Commons suggests a new way of stopping politicians gasbagging during Prime Minister's 'Question Time' because they know the cameras are on

TOO HONOURABLE: a man with no balls at all claims the moral high ground in Buckingham Palace; see also PIZZA EXPRESS

TOP PRIORITY: editor of *The Sun* tabloid explains pictorial policy during a staff meeting

TOTAL TOSSER: a caber-throwing Scotsman who hasn't touched a dram of whiskey in years; any member of the KKK

TOUPEE: a pair of bald Englishmen are ordered by a cranky Judge in a Chinese Communist Party Court Room to fork up for two wigs they tried to steal on a Tiananmen Square package holiday

TOWER OF LONDON: see IKEA Thurrock

TOY BOY: elderly lady mistakes a male model for a Tonka Truck

THROWING *HER* TOYS OUT OF THE PRAM: Einstein's granddaughter throws hissy fit in Hamleys Regent Street Toy Store due to (quote) 'easy-peasy' nature of Rubik Cubes

THROWING *HIS* TOYS OUT OF THE PRAM: Einstein's grandson throws his Rubik Cube at his sister to shut her up

TRACKING DEVICE: Amazon Prime is accused of going too far with its customer services for incontinent buyers by implanting a homing device in their arses that will deliver a bidet to their door in one-hour when a rectal urge is sensed

TRACKSUIT BOTTOMS: entire English Football Squad moons the gathered press photographers during a training session

TRAILER TRASH: any actress who exits Harvey Weinstein's on-set mobile home after a casting session who then forgets to sue for little things like rape after his role bagged her fame and glory and after which she subsequently attended red carpet events in a skimpy dress with her arms around Harvey Weinstein (both smiling) whilst both hog the limelight and spout words to appeasing interviewers about integrity and honesty and what a privilege it all was; a recruitment advert for Miramax Films; a bespoke welcome mat at Miramax Films

TRANSGENDER: alien that changes into shiny American cars and then talks like a street dude discovers he likes it both ways

TREASURE CHEST: actresses Elizabeth Hurley and Sydney Sweeney tell a glossy magazine where the money is

TRUPENNY BITS: Sophia Loren Spaghetti Recipe to improve chest size

TUPPAWARE: 60ts icon and fashion model Twiggy models a plastic dress for now people that attracts the opposite sex - and also has other helpful functions about the house

TWEET: A member of the Twat family; Tweety Bird sues electronic giants for the unauthorized use of his name in common message sending service

UNCONSCIOUS BIAS

U.F.O.: US Senator replies to a Ufologist looking for proof with a terse but pertinent rebuttal

UGANDAN DISCUSSIONS: a multi-lingual interpreter realizes her job application has been misread by the EU Orgy Committee in Brussels

ULTERIOR MOTIVE: locomotive with an agenda

UMBRAGE: a puzzled bridge

UMTEENTH REQUEST: a 16-year-old asking his parents for condoms (again)

UNABLE TO COMMENT: Abel refuses to speculate on his brother Kane's whereabouts to journalists from The Biblical Times

UNAVAILABLE FORMS: male University students complain about the lack of female models during life-drawing classes

UNBOSOMING SECRETS: Victoria Secret models undo their blouses in a trailer for the latest James Bond movie

UNCANNY RESEMBLENCE: a tin of peaches meets its twin

UNCOMMON VALOUR: Members of the House of Lords challenge the British Royal Family to open its fiscal accounts for public scrutiny

UNCONSCIOUS BIAS: the morning after, and still asleep, a hungover Millwall supporter lying prostate on the floor of Ali Baba's Kebab Emporium mutters something untoward and even defamatory about the cuisine at Ali's the night before he passed out

UNCONTROLLABLE OUTCOME: a penis admits to a vagina that without his usual sheath protection, things might get a bit gushy later on

UNDERACHIEVER: BJ given beneath a desk at a *Be Your Best Self* Seminar

UNDERDOG: Alsatian is surprised to find a Chiwawa making overtures beneath the hood

UNDERFLOOR HEATING: a lagged waterpipe gets horny for a kitchen tile

UNDERLAY: Boris Johnson makes out with Theresa May beneath London Bridge in a virtually silent Toyota Prius whilst their driver takes both to the Carpet Right half-price sale to pick out new Axminster for 10 Downing Street: a technical phrase describing sexual intercourse between moles

UNDULATING LANDSCAPE: male realtor looking down Pamela Anderson's blouse comments on locations assets

UNEXPECTED ROCK FORMATION: Dwayne Johnson on the Baywatch set

UPSET THE APPLE CART: A Trolley in the Cardiac Ward of Whipp's Cross Hospital is given two weeks compassionate leave after being stampeded during a recent delivery of Royal Galas and Golden Delicious

URANIAN RESERVES: Russian Nuclear Material admits using political influence to book seats for the London Opera House

URBAN MYTH: to gain credibility amongst academics in the storytelling community, a fairy-tale bump ups his street cred by wearing hoodies and trainers and singing rap

USER ID: nametag given to Heroin Junkies at the Betty Ford Clinic

VIKING TRAIL

VACATION HOTSPOT: on their honeymoon in yet another lavishly decorated tent, Delilah finger points Samson at an area likely to produce familial results

THE VAGINA MONOLOGUES: - a Vladivostok housewife drops her knickers in November and discovers that at 40-below, her labia is quoting Tolstoy to stay warm

DICK VAN DYKE: a crossdressing Van Morrison tribute act; after seeing sunflowers sensually swaying in a Dutch field, mad artist Vincent Van Gogh became sexually aroused and wrote to his brother Theo immediately demanding money for a sex-change

VALHALLA: the name of a very hardwearing type of IKEA floor laminate that covers all the approach paths to the Pearly Gates when you die (the Swedes get everywhere)

VALUE ADDED TAX: a Soho lady of the night demands a tip from the British Chancellor of the Exchequer on a boy's night out in the West End

VENTILATION DUCT: World Record Holder for rapid flatulence spares his audience by placing a flap to the outside carpark in his pants

VIKING TRAIL: a long line of dark-haired European women with an even longer line of red and blond-haired children

VISIONARY: Delilah shows Samson what makes him want to excitedly knock down temple pillars

VOCAL CORDS: singing trousers made in the Seventies; husband's Seventies trousers that still serenade other women while the wife isn't looking

VOLUME CONTROL: having pointed Samson to her vacation hotspot, Delilah now has to ask her man to tone down the hollers

WANG DANG DOODLE

WALL-MOUNTED FAN: Sydney Sweeny hangs another crazed male admirer on her condo wall

WANG DANG DOODLE: scribbles in the sketchpad of Wang Dang, a Japanese Anime artist: Texan oil tycoon Hoyt Wangford dangles his penis at passers-by after he's finished urinating on one of his oil pumps

WAR GAMES: Supreme Leader Kim Jong-un of North Korea describes his children's absolute favourite playtime activity (with real tanks and missile silos)

WATER SPORTS: secretary finds out that after coming home with her drunken boss from the Christmas party and sleeping with him, he wasn't talking about Jet Skis when he talked at the party about what he wanted

WELL ENDOWED: a watering-hole with huge pumps; English Aristocratic Lady marries a Thai Mail Order Prince but is disappointed to find that he was referring to a cavernous watering hole in his back garden and not impressive personal equipment; wishing well leaving a physical fitness centre: Disney Wishing Well drops his pants in an enchanted forest and makes a shocking revelation to Snow White

WELL-ESTABLISHED: smart Bedouin camel leads its rider to a well-known watering hole in the Sahara Desert

WHERE ANGELS FEAR TO TREAD: Charlie's Angels cancel a crochet class after its ex-KGB teacher stabs a student in the eye for dropping a stitch on a Vladamir Putin themed baby-grow; Gary Glitter's dressing room

WHIG OUT: a toupee goes on a date

WHISTLE DOWN THE WIND: an Opera Singer tries to control a farting fit
WIDE-BODIED JETS: entire American Football Team puts on a little too much weight

WHOPPERS: a DD bra lunching in Burgerking

WICKERWORK: a basket case looking for a job

WIDELY HELD BELIEFS: largest man in the world claims he knows God as he hugs a priest; 1000 cream cakes get religion

WIFE: a woman who used to say you were good in bed but now won't talk to you at all unless technically/legally necessary; style adjudicator on the rare occasion you're allowed to shop for clothes in M&S, unaccompanied

WILLY WONKA: NHS Doctor gives a curveball diagnosis to pensioner; British Royal Family doctors help Prince Charles after his 70th birthday party celebrations go awry in November 2018 and find that his penis has been covered in dark chocolate and tied in a Windsor knot

WITH KNOBS ON: Old Compton Street Night Club entices gay patrons and Liberal Democrats with the chance to wear dresses covered in male genitalia; London estate agent bigs up extras on the door of a dog kennel selling for a piffling £349,995

WOBBLY BITS: computer data program wearing a tight dress

WOEBEGONE: a manic depressive is asked to leave therapy

WOLF WHISTLES: A werewolf learns the flute; Howlin' Wolf watches his wife shimmy into the bedroom

WOODPILES: a sycamore tree with haemorrhoids

WORDS FAIL ME: Former US Democrat President Joe Biden's stock reply to any question on money or anything other subject for that matter (see also DENIES ALL KNOWLEDGE)

WORK TO RULE: a Geometry Set goes on strike

WUNDERBAR: first German pub on Mars

"NO, AUNT FANNY – I SAID HE'S SHOWING HIS PRIZE BULLOCKS AT THE COUNTRY FAIR."

X-RAY SPECS

X BOX 360: championship Boxer is disqualified because the authorities found eyes in the back of his head

X CHROMOSOME: gene trait organism (XX) breaks it off with her longstanding boyfriend (XY)

X MARKS THE SPOT: (aka ARSEHOLE): disgruntled mum of a rejected X-Factor contestant holds Simon Cowell hostage in local LYDL supermarket, only to force him to draw the cross-letter on his bare bottom and put his money where his mouth is

X RATED: alphabet letter X receives a sexual thumbs-up from his wife Y

X-RAY: one of Ray Charles' old girlfriends

X-RAY SPECS: a set of Ray Charles' discarded sunglasses

X-RAY TUBE: a box of Smarties once owned by Ray Charles

XANADU: Anne Boylyn considers remarrying Henry the VIII

XENOPHOBIA: Buddah has an allergic reaction in a trance

XEROX: a photocopier on holiday sends a postcard home from The Rocky Mountains

XTC: a former-drug user at The Daily Telegraph's Crossword Puzzle section

XYLOPHONE: a coinbox in a US missile silo

YIELD NOT TO TEMPTATION

YABBA DABBA DOO: mating call of Fred Flintstone to his wife

YABBI: Jewish Cleric on a Yacht

YACHT ROCK: Dwayne Johnson on a schooner

YAH YAH: hooray Henry hipster with an annoying habit of repeating himself

YAR!: ZZ Top's new album

YARDBIRD: a lady convict strolls past the men's section

YARDIRON: male convicts watch her stroll past

YE OF LITTLE FAITH – A Termite Mound at Prayer

YEARLY PROJECTIONS: Annual General Meeting laying out the number of ejaculation shots needed in the Adult Entertainment industry

YELLOW PEARL: Having been given the wrong colour bottle of hair dye, President Donald Trump stands over the nuclear launch codes in a rage

YELLOW SUBMARINE: a patriotic banana wants the British Royal Navy to paint one of their nuclear hunter-killer submersibles a distinctive colour; Russian Navy repays the Beatles "Back In The U.S.S.R" song by painting one their atomic powered submersibles in a certain colour and adorning the turret with a plaque that says "we all live in a..."

YELLOWBILL: a receipt given at a Jaundice Clinic

YELLOWWOOD: a US Park Ranger with an erection

YESTERDAY AND TODAY: British scientists in Liverpool finally admit that Beatles song sounds good no matter what day of the week you hear it

YIELD NOT TO TEMPTATION: Adam's *unpublished* autobiography

YIKES: environmentally-friendly motorbikes for Yuppies

YIPPIE: an excited Hippie

YOB ELEMENT: a Russell Hobbs Kettle breaks bad

YODELING PRACTICE: Doorbell ringtone at an Alpine Medical Centre

YOGHURTS: what novices say after their first session with a Yoga Guru

YOGI BEAR: a Grizzly discovers Transcendental Meditation

YOKIBOB: an egg called Robert at a loose end

YORKSHIRE PUDDING: Michael Parkinson's nickname for his aging arse

YOU TAKE THE HIGH ROAD: knowing the low path takes you to an Aztec city containing more jewels and gold than God, smiling but sweaty Amazonian guide advises well-dressed treasure hunters from New York to try an alternate route

YOUNGBLOODS: Dracula's offspring

YOUNGSTERS: the children of hipsters; offspring of psychiatrist Carl Jung

YOUTHFUL FOLLY: two-year old white infant in Alabama is inspired after seeing a Republican rally on television and immediately tries to build a 100-foot-high wall in his back garden to keep out Mexicans and caravans filled with strong men (see CARAVAN)

YUCKY: nickname given by Lucky the Dog to his excrement

YULETIDE GREETINGS: a Christmas Card from a Tsunami

ZING WENT THE STRINGS OF MY HEART

ZAPPED: a Frank Zappa app

ZEALOT: fanatical bids at an auction

ZEBRA: a stripped brassiere in Germany

ZEN STATE: Peace announces its intentions for World Peace

ZERO HOURS CONTRACT: the *minute-hand* in a Swiss Watch is sued by his workmate the *hour-hand* for having better pay conditions

ZERO VISIBILITY: larger-than-life Jewish comedic actor Zero Mostel fails to hide from Director Mel Brooks when casting his film "The Producers"; Japanese fighter plane is pursued by an American Typhoon into the clouds over Tokyo

ZERO TOLERANCE: the Number One finally admits to his abhorrence of the digit that preceded him after he casually broke his heart at the Mensa Mathematics Prom night

ZIGGY STARDUST: after a visit to the 1989 set of "Baywatch", self-aware AI called Ziggy in the 1993 TV show "Quantum Leap" starring Scott Bakula and Dean Stockwell about body transportation through time finds a dune of galactic sand in its circuitry; staggeringly inventive David Bowie character from 1972

ZIGZAG: name of David Bowie's pet Jaguar

ZING WENT THE STRINGS OF MY HEART: On the Forbidden Planet, Robby The Robot falls in love with the inside of a piano

ZIPPITY DOO DAH: a Member of the Bonzo Dg Doo Dah Band does up his fly after having a tinkle

ZOOLOGICAL SOCIETY: London Zoo allows Spock of Star Trek free membership

LEFT LUGGAGE SERIES of Paperbacks and E-Books

BY MARK BARRY

LEFT LUGGAGE Series (Poems and Limericks - Books 1 to 9)
Book 1 - MY BROKEN HEART (75 Days In The NHS)
Book 2 - SIGNIFICANT OTHERS
Book 3 - UNDECIDED JINNY JOE
Book 4 - RESONATOR
Book 5 - SHARP INHALE (Love Poems and Thereabouts)
Book 6 - SICK KITTENS TO WARM BRICKS
Book 7 - ADAM WAKES UP IN THE GARDEN OF EDEN WITH A FIERCE PAIN IN HIS SIDE
      (The Wonders of Men - Parts 1 to 122)
Book 8 - HIMMLER HAD SOMETHING SIMILAR (100 Limericks Volume 1)
Book 9 - FOR A FEW LIMERICKS MORE (100 Limericks Volume 2)

LEFT LUGGAGE Series (Words and Phrases with Witty Explanations from A to Z)
Book 10 - A QUICK SHUFTY...And Other Popular Outdoor Activities

LEFT LUGGAGE Series (Poem Compendiums)
Book 11 - CLEARING UP AHEAD (A Shorter Version of *Significant Others*)
Book 12 - TROUBLING DEAF HEAVEN (Compendium of Poems Books 1 to 9)
Book 14 - BRIGHT BLAST MORNING (Compendium of Autism/Carer Poems 1 to 9)

LEFT LUGGAGE Series (Screenplays)
Book 13 - THE CLOTHS OF HEAVEN (1990s Northern Ireland Peace Process)
Book 15 - SILAS (A Politician's Journey Back from the Loss of his Son)
Book 16 - AN ENGLISH LADY
(Life Story of Eglantyne Louisa Jebb, Founder of the Save The Children Fund)
Book 17 - FULL OF GRACE
(Love Story around the 9/11 New York atrocities as a way of National Healing)

LEFT LUGGAGE Series (Film and TV Reviews)
Book 18 - KEEPERS and SLEEPERS
(Movies You Probably Haven't Seen And Some You Should Own)

INTERNET REFERENCES
AMAZON UK - Hall of Fame Reviewer Six Times – Over 2.5 Million Views
AMAZON AUTHOR'S PAGE
Type the following into any Search Engine - B00LQKMC6I

SOUNDS GOOD, LOOKS GOOD Blogger Site
2,760-Plus, Posts and Reviews - Over 2.75 Million Views
Copy the following into any Search Engine
https://markattheflicks.blogspot.com/

ALSO BY MARK BARRY

The *Sounds Good Music Books* Series (32 Titles)
All-Genre Guides to Exceptional CD Reissues and Remasters
Available on all AMAZON Sites as Downloadable e-Books

YEAR Volumes
VOODOO CHILE – 1968
WHOLE LOTTA LOVE – 1969
ALL THINGS MUST PASS – 1970
GET IT ON – 1971
TUMBLING DICE – 1972
US AND THEM – 1973
PICK UP THE PIECES – 1974
CAPT. FANTASTIC – 1975
MORE THAN A FEELING – 1976
PROVE IT ALL NIGHT – 1977 to 1979

DECADE Volumes
GIMME SHELTER! - Classic 1960s Rock & Pop
ALL RIGHT NOW – Classic Rock & Pop 1970 – 1974 – A to L
REASON TO BELIEVE – Classic Rock & Pop 1970 to 1974 – M to Z
LET'S GO CRAZY – 1980s Music on CD – Exceptional CD Remasters

GENRE Volumes
CADENCE / CASCADE – Prog, Psych, Avant Garde (1966 to 1976)
SOUL GALORE! – 60ts Soul, 60ts R&B, Northern, Mod, New Breed,
Rare Groove
HIGHER GROUND – 70ts Soul, Funk and Jazz Fusion
BOTH SIDES NOW – 1960s and 1970s Folk & Country Music & Rock
Thereabouts
MANNISH BOY – Blues, Rhythm 'n' Blues, Vocal Groups, Doo Wop &
Rockabilly

THEMED Volumes
SOMETHING'S HAPPENING HERE Volumes 1 to 7 – 1960's & 1970s (7 Books)
I SAW THE LIGHT – Overlooked Albums 1955 to 1979 (500-plus titles)
LOOKING AFTER NO. 1 – Debut Albums 1956 to 1986 Vol. 1 – A to L
LOOKING AFTER NO. 1 – Debut Albums 1956 to 1986 Vol. 2 – M to Z
URGE TO SPLURGE – The First Ten Years Of Double-Albums 1966 to 1976
BOXING CLEVER - Best CD Box Sets Ever
GOODY TWO SHOES – Best 2CD Deluxe Editions and Anthologies

MY BROKEN HEART
(75 Days In The NHS)

A Poem A Day

A Quad Bi-Pass

A Second Chance...

MARK
BARRY

Paperback £9.95 on Amazon

SIGNIFICANT OTHERS

Poems
Dublin, London, Margate

MARK BARRY

Paperback £9.95 on Amazon

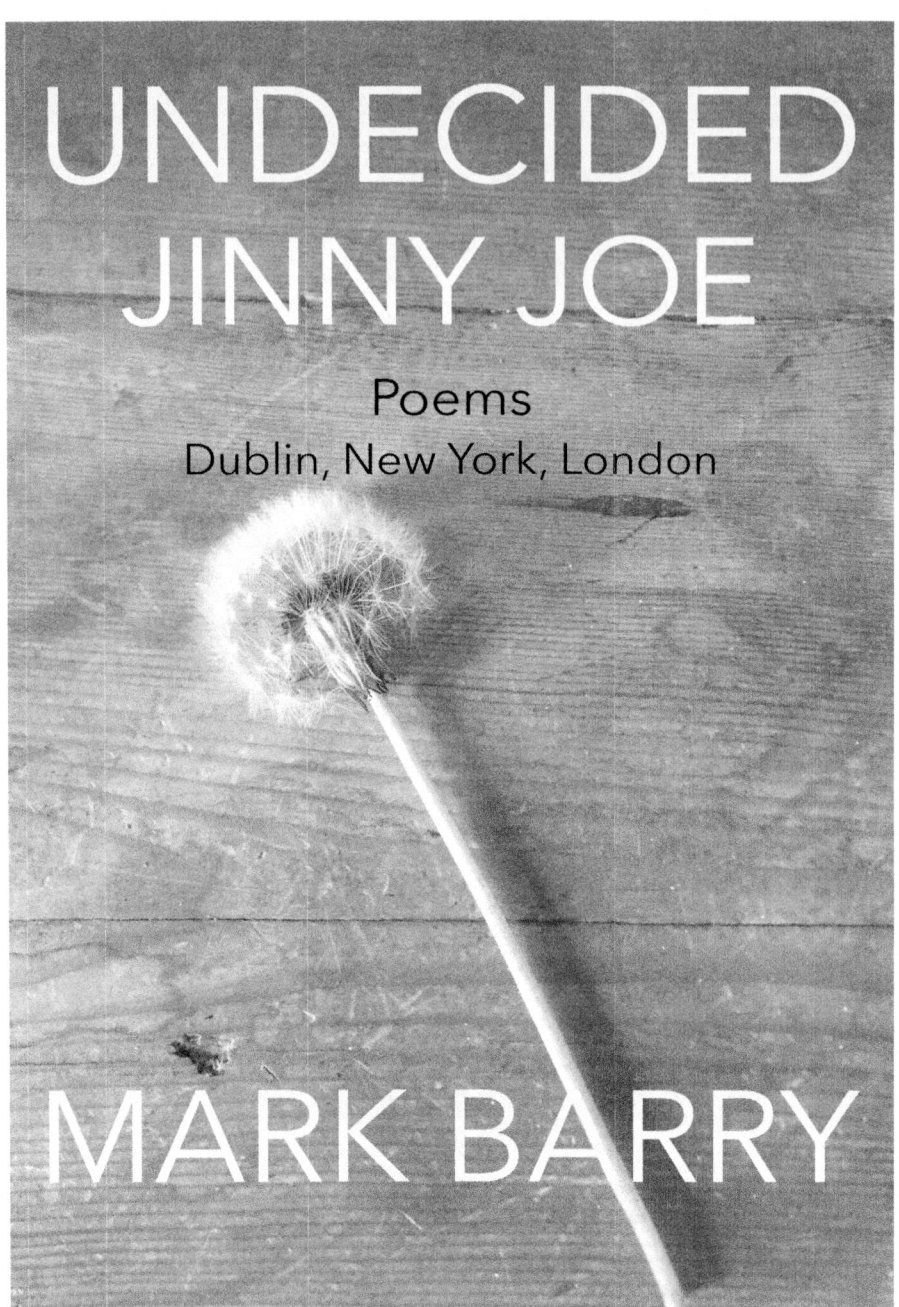

UNDECIDED
JINNY JOE

Poems
Dublin, New York, London

MARK BARRY

Paperback £9.95 on Amazon

SICK KITTENS TO WARM BRICKS

POEMS

MARK BARRY

Paperback £9.95 on Amazon

Paperback £9.95 on Amazon

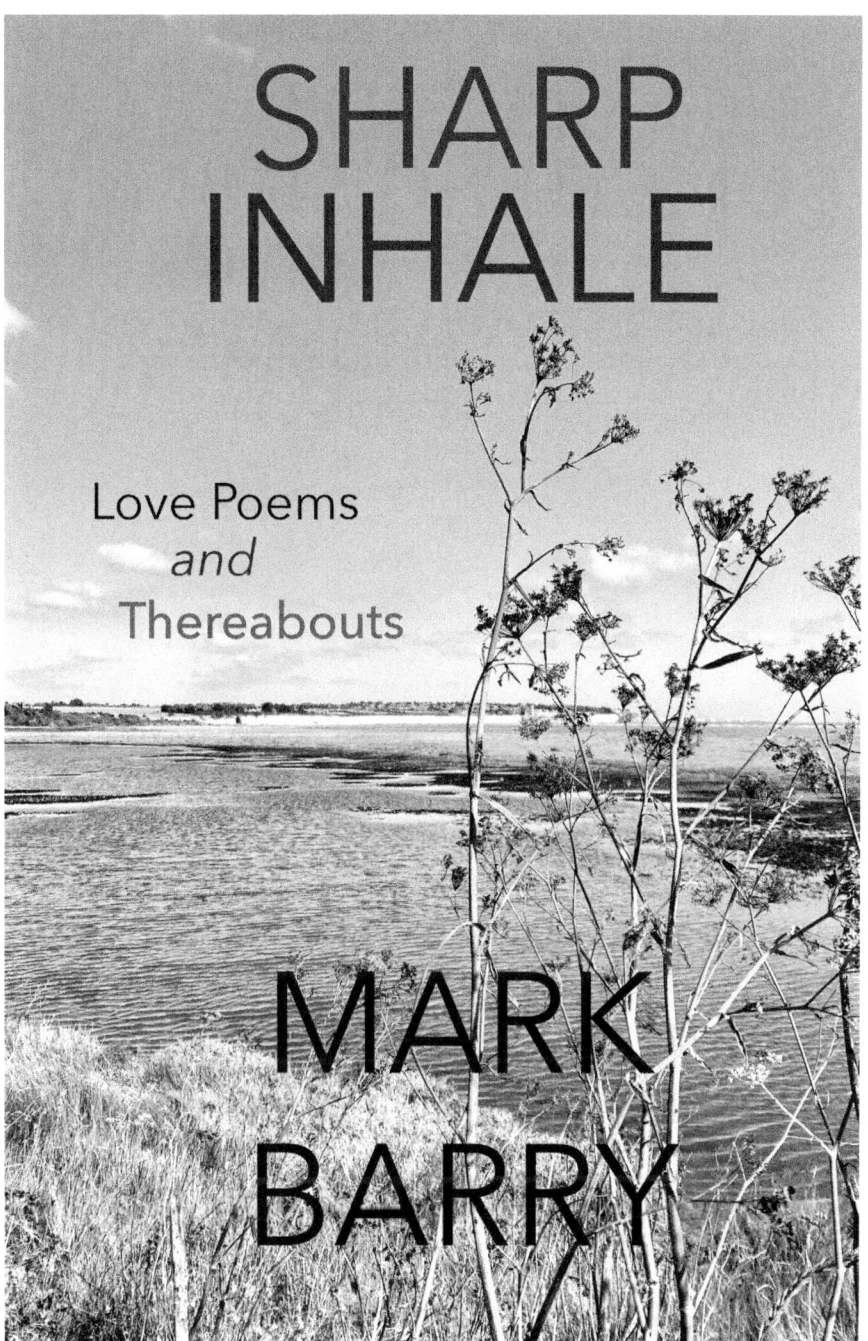

SHARP
INHALE

Love Poems
and
Thereabouts

MARK
BARRY

Paperback £9.95 on Amazon

HIMMLER HAD SOMETHING SIMILAR

(Two, But They Were Small)

**Limericks For One-Hundred Cultural Miscreants
And Other Historically *Supple* Characters**

MARK BARRY

Paperback £9.95 on Amazon

ADAM WAKES UP
IN THE
GARDEN OF EDEN...

Or One Chap's Journey To *Lurve And Happiness*
Through The Interpretive Medium of Rhyming Verse

MARK BARRY

Paperback £9.95 on Amazon

FOR A FEW
LIMERICKS
MORE

Another One-Hundred Cultural Miscreants
And *Historically Flexible* Characters

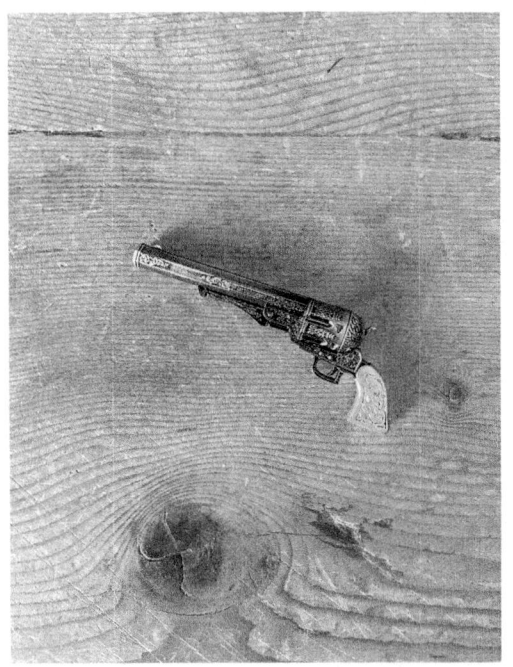

MARK BARRY

Paperback £9.95 on Amazon

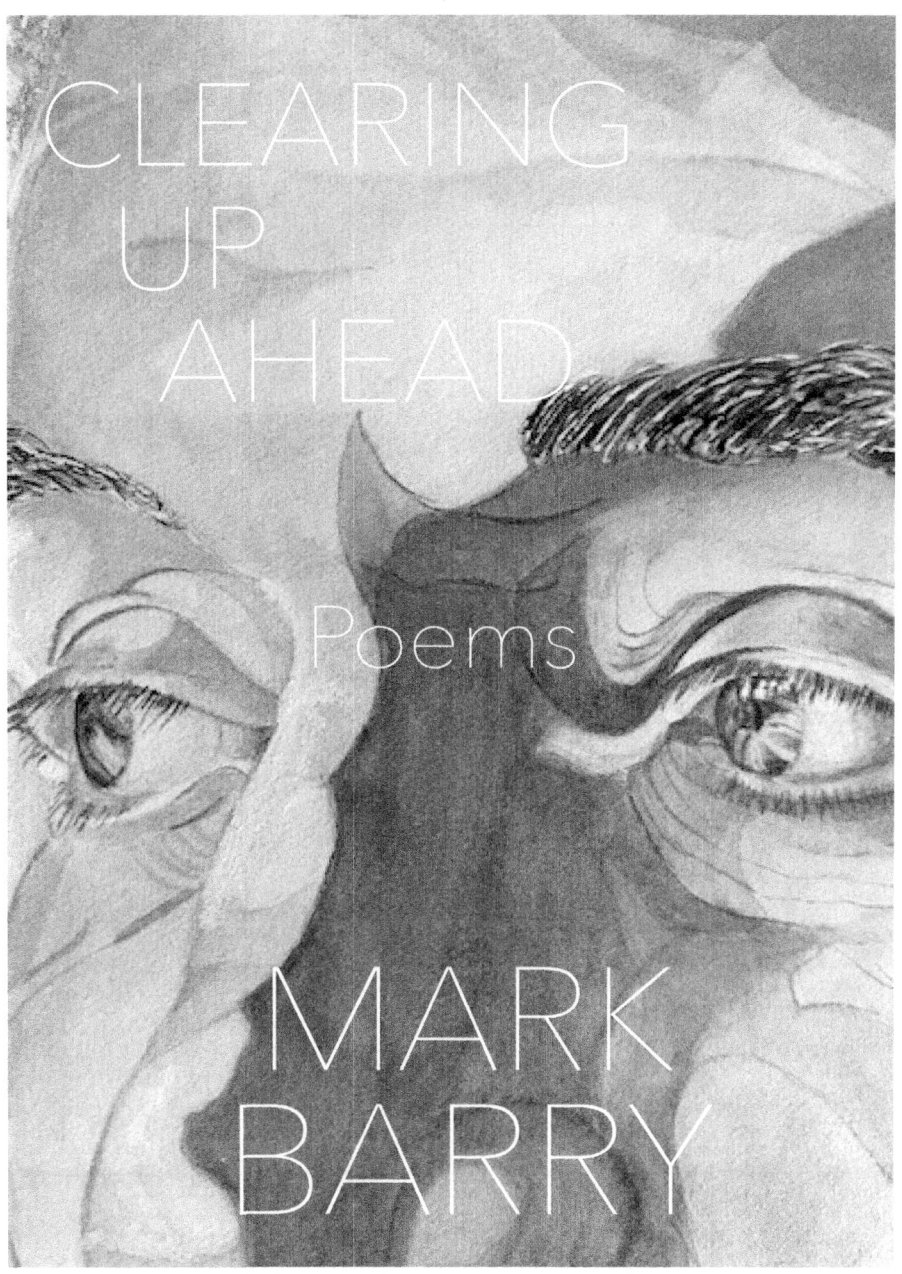

CLEARING UP AHEAD

Poems

MARK BARRY

Paperback £9.95 on Amazon
(Shorter Version of *Significant Others*)

TROUBLING
DEAF HEAVEN

Poems

MARK
BARRY

Compendium of Poems from *Books 1 to 9*
Paperback £9.95 on Amazon

BRIGHT BLAST MORNING

Poems About An Autistic Son
Four Decades of Special Needs

MARK BARRY

Paperback £9.95 on Amazon

The Cloths of Heaven

A Screenplay About The Back-Channels
In the Northern Ireland Peace Process 1994

MARK BARRY

Screenplay in Paperback £14.95 on Amazon

Amazon E-Book of 3,177 pages, available as a download £4.95

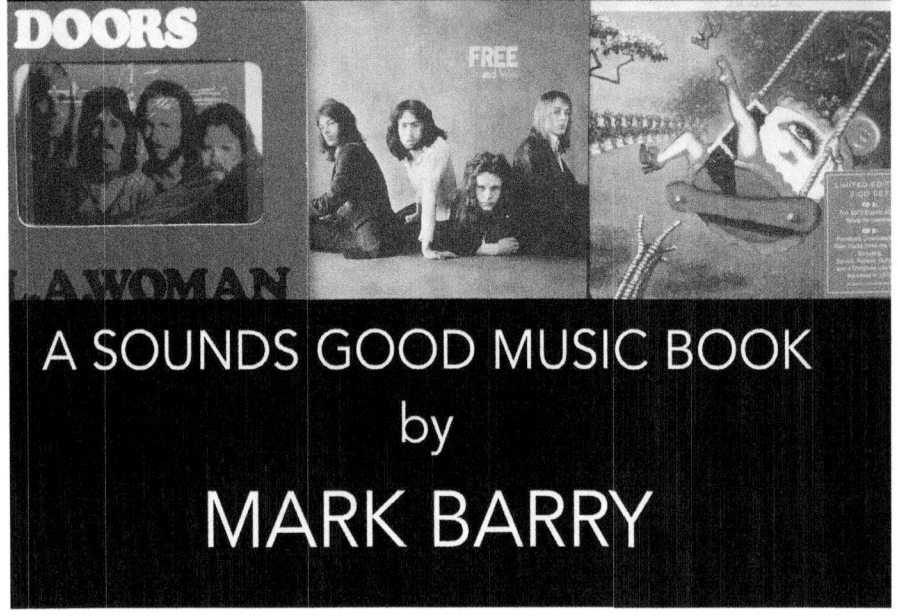

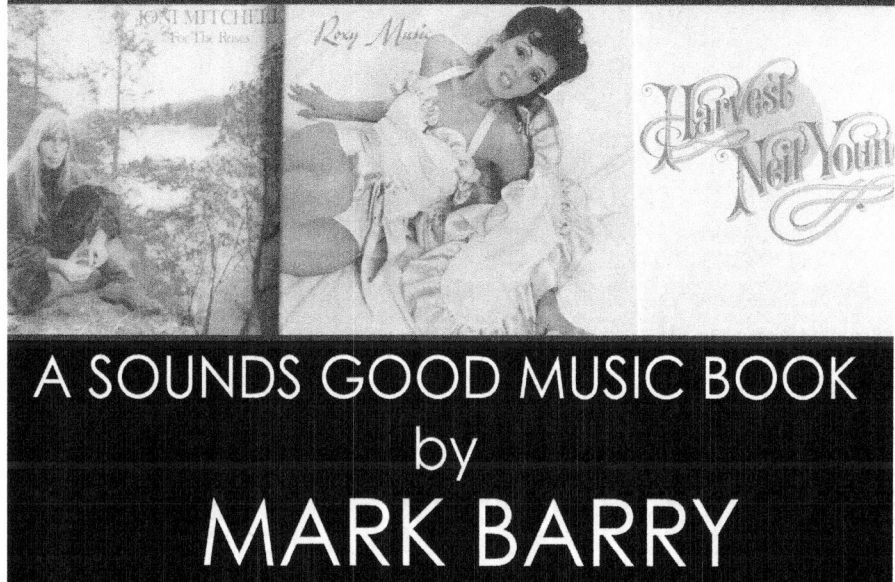

PROVE IT ALL NIGHT

Music of 1977 to 1979

Your GuideTo Exceptional
CD Reissues & Remasters...

A SOUNDS GOOD MUSIC BOOK
by
MARK BARRY

Amazon E-Book of 2,118 pages, available as a download £4.95

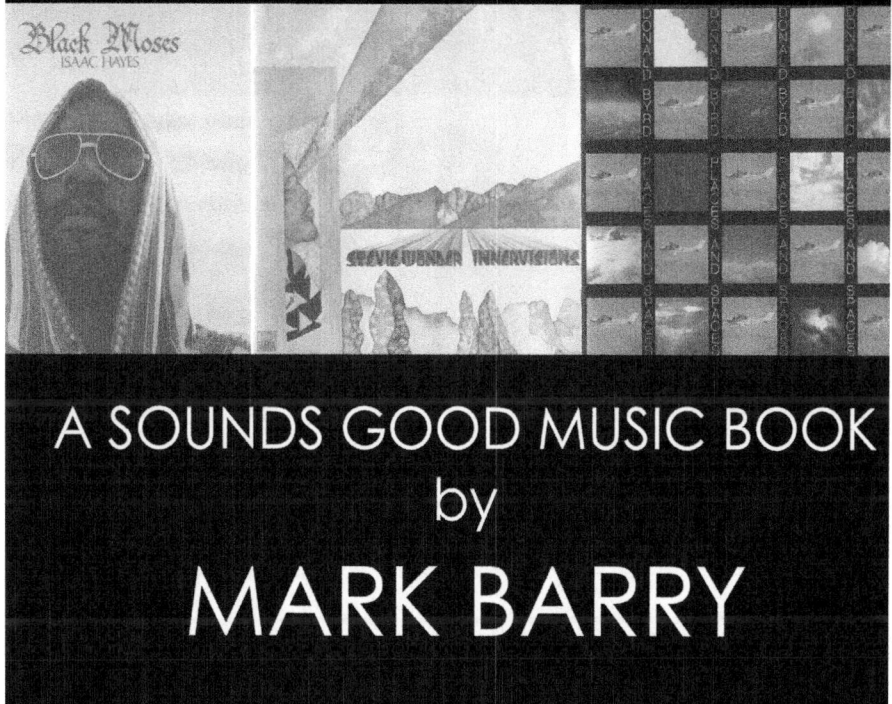

Amazon E-Book of 2,234 pages, available as a download £4.95

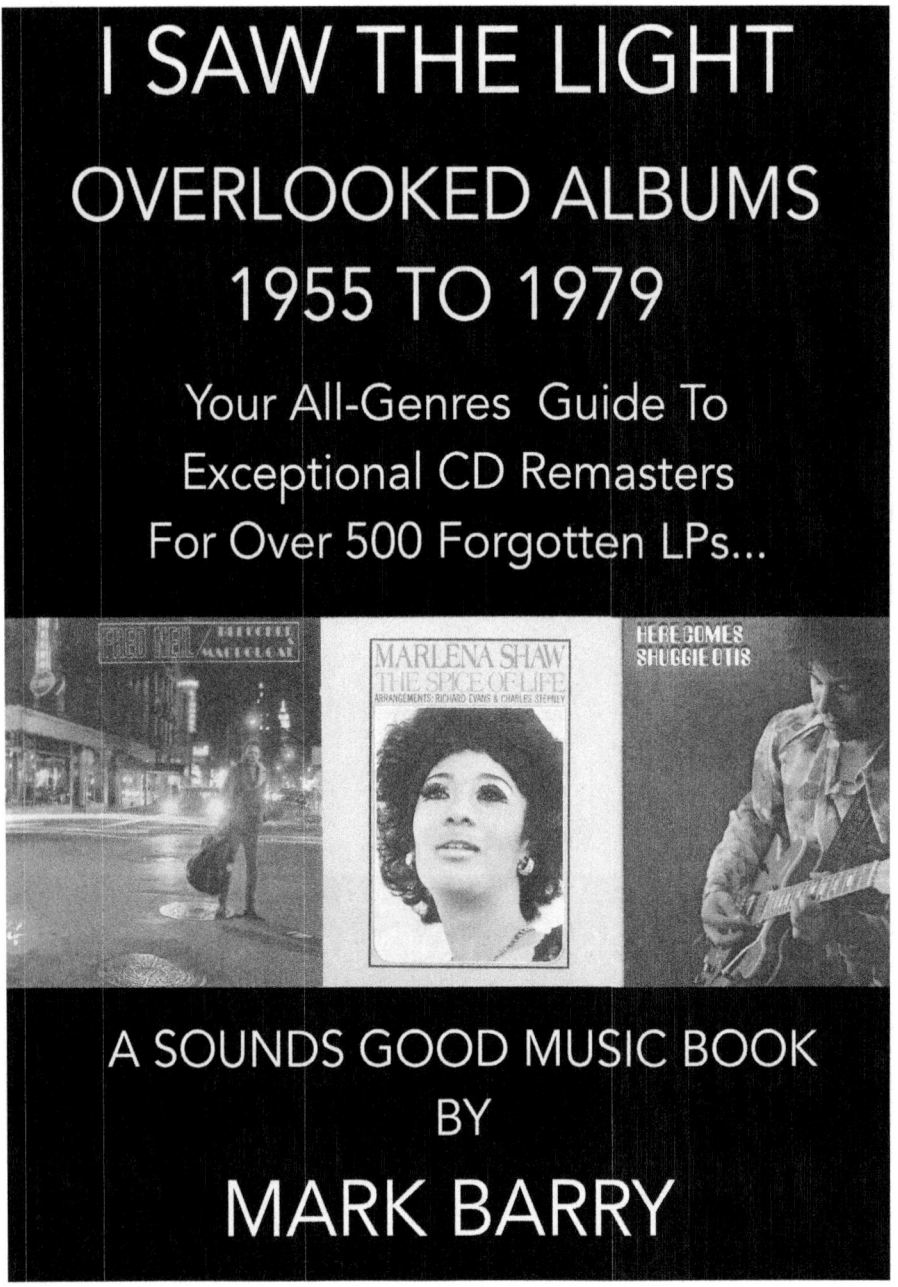

I SAW THE LIGHT

OVERLOOKED ALBUMS
1955 TO 1979

Your All-Genres Guide To
Exceptional CD Remasters
For Over 500 Forgotten LPs...

A SOUNDS GOOD MUSIC BOOK
BY
MARK BARRY

Amazon E-Book of 3,096 pages, available as a download £7.95

Amazon E-Book of 1,793 pages, available as a download £4.95

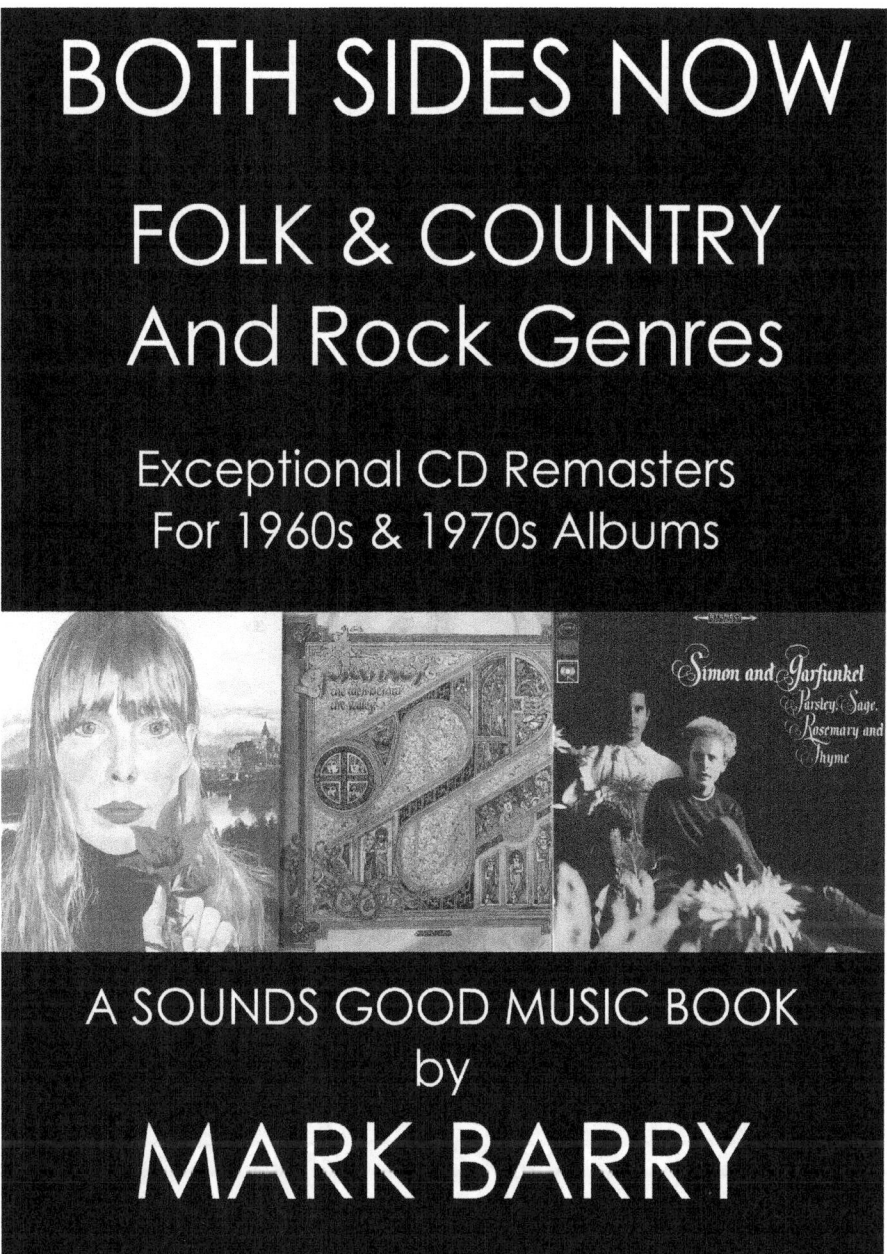

Amazon E-Book of 1,348 pages, available as a download £4.95

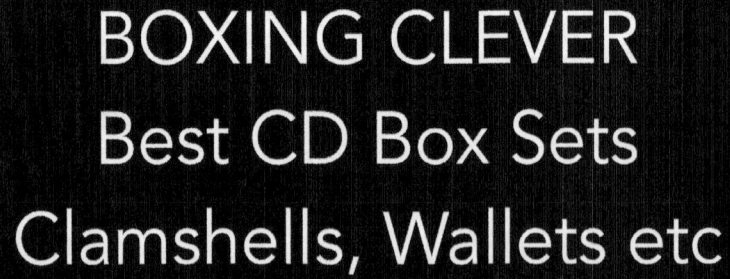

Amazon E-Book of 3,002 pages, available as a download £4.95

Printed in Dunstable, United Kingdom